JOHN LORY

Waiting At The Dock

JOHN LORY

Waiting At The Dock

John Lory

JOHN LORY

Waiting At The Dock

He waited at the dock.

One day his ship would come in.

So, he waited at the dock.

Time passed.

Behind him was the better half of life; over, gone, locked forever in time's vault. Ahead of him was the other half of life; an unknown journey with an inevitable outcome.

The ship.

Was it yet to arrive? Had he missed it? Was there no ship at all?

Time passed.

He waited at the dock.

Contents

Down The Line... 9
Men For The Ages... 17
A Matter Of Time.. 23
Spirit Of '73... 35
The Disappearance of David Conroy..................... 39
All Gone... 57
Smart Josef... 63
The Three Forces.. 81
Johnny Lee Dillard.. 87
The Catch Of A Lifetime................................. 101
The Electric Man.. 113
The Fink.. 123
The Purple Navigator..................................... 133
Sunset..137
My Brother Dimas..159

Down The Line

He needed to pee.

This was a problem for him because he'd lose his place in the line. And, he stood in the line simply because he'd lost all originality and uniqueness in his life. He'd become a lemming; a cookie-cutter gingerbread man rolling off the assembly line; a tall thin tree standing in the middle of a hundred acres of other tall thin trees.

This line that he was standing in slithered into a brightly lit store that had just received a shipment of the newest and hottest phone on planet earth. He needed this phone with a fruit logo on the back of it because, well, that's *what everybody else was getting*. He'd been in a very similar line, at the same store, about 8 months earlier, just to get the fruit phone that had been all the rage *back then*. Now he was back.

Come to think of it, he'd been spending lots of precious time inching forward in lines, uncomfortably sandwiched between strangers to the front and back. Always waiting, always anticipating, always his mind focused on whatever morsel of temporary delight awaited him when he finally reached the front.

He had failed to notice what had happened to him. The merry-go-round his life had become. So caught up in living a status symbol life. Always trying to get ahead, always trying to be the subject of envy. Not only keeping up with the Joneses but getting *ahead of them* and *everybody else on the block*.

The things he'd done.

The day after Thanksgiving. Black Friday. He'd wallow out of bed, leaving his little cocoon of warmth, and pile into the previous day's clothes lying on the floor. Swill around a shot glass of peppermint oral rinse in his sticky mouth, grab a granola bar, bundle up, and scurry out the door to Wal-Mart to stand in a line, under the stars, on a crisp November morn. And he'd wait. Jostled and bumped by the unfriendlies in the line; listening to them yapping and bitching about the weather and musing aloud about the odds of those *"Wal-Mart bastards"* opening the doors in the next ten minutes.

Then the time would arrive. The moment the doors opened. The crowd would surge like a rogue wave advancing on a quiet fishing village. Elbows were thrown, nasty epitaphs were uttered, and the young and meek were rolled.

One year it was a Furby. A must-have that year, and he was determined to get one. To become one of the elites who'd claimed one of the fabulous toys. His quest to get one hadn't been pretty. It involved a footrace, a well-timed vault over a half-pallet of dog food, a little blonde girl who he may or may not have tripped, and a short but close quarters tugging match with a heavyweight woman in a dirty purple windbreaker. It wasn't his proudest moment, but he came out the owner of a Furby.

Then there was Star Wars. Revenge of the Sith to be exact. Midnight showing to be even more exact. Another line. This one courtesy of the local paper. Lacking credible news to report, they had broadcast the midnight showing of Revenge of the Sith on the front page. Then, using space on page two, they'd interviewed Mikey Goddard, the self-described *biggest Star Wars fan in the*

WAITING AT THE DOCK

area. Mikey was going to camp out in front of the local cinema starting at 4 PM and be the first person to get a ticket at the stroke of midnight. Other dorks thought this a good idea and hence began the line. Not surprisingly, he'd been one of the *other* dorks.

He'd stood outside the cinema, leaning against a brick wall, a blue ball cap hiding his face from the glaring May sunshine. Dorks talked to each other while waiting. How did Anakin become Vader? How did Yoda end up in a swamp? If Jar-Jar had a major part they might just walk out of the theater right then in there. Make a bold statement to Lucas about their displeasure in the direction of the blasted storyline.

Cars drove by; people coming and going from work. Many gave the dorks curious or disapproving stares. He tried to tell himself that they were just jealous--jealous that they wouldn't be some of the first to see the new movie. Second place citizens, they'd be. He listened as Mikey Goddard chewed his way through a large bag of puffy Cheetos and power slammed 20 oz Mountain Dew.

Were the people in the cars really jealous?

He knew little about Star Wars and didn't care how Yoda ended up in a swamp, but yet, he was in line. On the cutting edge of a worldwide event. One of the very first to witness this new, sure-to-be, record-setting cinematic spectacle. He could brag about it at work. Yeah, the new Star Wars movie? I've already seen it.

Movie time. He tiredly sat in his theater seat at a quarter past midnight. A stormtrooper on one side; Obi-Wan and his musty smelling robes on the other. The whole place mirrored a Halloween party. Mikey Goddard was in front of him. He'd gotten his hands on another bag of Cheetos.

11

He fell asleep about a half-hour into the movie. Didn't get to see how Vader came about or Yoda moving to the swamp. When he awoke the last of the credits were running. The place was nearly deserted. He tripped over the stormtrooper's empty popcorn box as he exited the row.

Then there was the time Mark Miller came to town. A brief stopover to meet, greet, sign autographs, and take pictures. A bonafide, dyed-in-wool celebrity of all things! He'd be at the YMCA from 1:30 to 3:00. Another line to get into.

Wicked little pellets of ice stung his red, wind bitten cheeks as he waited his turn in the slippery YMCA parking lot. The two middle-aged ladies in front of him were sure excited that Mark Miller was inside, at a folding table, only a few hundred feet away. They regaled each other with tales of all the Sawyer Brown concerts they'd attended. One had been backstage in Cedar Rapids or some such place. She'd met Mark Miller that night and wondered if he'd remember her. The other one had VIP tickets once but had to sell them on craigslist because her boss was a major jerk who wouldn't let her off work. The company sure didn't get her best effort that night, she groused.

He didn't know that Mark Miller was the lead singer of the band, Sawyer Brown. He knew nothing about him. But, this was a happening. Others would talk about the event. He could say he'd been there. That he'd met Mark Miller.

His ears ached from the cold when he finally got inside the building. He peeked up to the front of the line. A table. A chair. A stack of 8x10 glossy photos, but no Mr. Mark Miller.

A big guy with really hairy arms and a giant gut waddled out. Time was up. Thanks for coming out. Mark Miller needed to get to Milwaukee for tonight's show. He'd signed a bunch of photos and everybody was going to get one.

A rumble of displeasure rippled through the line of about twenty people as Big Guy shuffled past, handing out glossies. One lady said the whole thing sucked. Another claimed some kind of scam was being run. A gangly guy refused to take a photo because the whole thing was just bullshit. Big guy ignored them all.

He left the YMCA that day with a signed, grayscale, studio-quality picture of a smiling Mark Miller wearing a cowboy hat. It went into his paper recycling a couple of days later.

And this brought him back to the line he was currently standing in. Doing what it took to get ahead of those elusive Joneses.

Eventually, he'd get inside. Eventually, he'd give $850.00 to some mid-twenties guy who had spiked hair and smelled of Old Spice. And then... he'd get *the phone* that the rest of the world wanted. He could bring it out at work. Yep, got this beauty just last night.

He uncomfortably shifted his weight trying to alleviate the pressure on his overtaxed bladder. He watched through the windows into the shiny store, envisioning himself at the head of the line. Watched as others plunked down their money and got a white box with the fruit logo on the front of it. Watched as they exited the store all excited, noses stuck to their new purchase.

A dude in a leather jacket bumped him from behind, spiking his growing discomfort. He looked back and gave the oblivious guy a nasty glare. The line moved ahead two feet.

Leather jacket dude bumped him again. Jerk. He wanted to turn and belt the inconsiderate guy in his greasy face. Instead, he pulled out his 8-month-old phone and turned it on; peered at the screen. It was a really nice phone; still looked new.

Then, impulse gently nipped at him. Then again, only harder. What in hell was he doing? Why was he in this line? Why hadn't he used the bathroom earlier? He grew irritated and suddenly, without the slightest tingle of regret, he stepped out of line.

Nobody noticed or cared.

Across the street was a small Mobil station. He went inside and made a beeline towards the bathrooms. No line! He stood at the urinal, his misery draining away. Tears welled in his eyes. Sweet relief!

Exiting the bathroom he felt like a different man. Like a million bucks. Sure the empty bladder was part of it, but he felt something else, something more. Something more profound; like a huge yoke had been lifted off of his shoulders.

He looked around the well-lit convenience store. It was desolate. He went to the soda fountain. No line at the soda fountain. He filled a giant, festive, plastic cup to the brim with Mountain Dew. He then walked over to the candy aisle. No line in the candy aisle. He grabbed a king-size bag of peanut M&M's. He went to the checkout. No line at the checkout. He paid and was on his way.

He stepped out of the store, stood under the overhang, and slurped his drink.

 It started to rain. Steady drizzle soon followed by fat heavy drops.

He saw that the people across the street, in the phone store line, were gripped with indecision and confusion. What to do? Where to go? Some flattened against the windows of the store, making themselves as thin as possible, hoping the narrow ledge above them would provide protection. Some burst towards the front door--a surge like Black Friday. Others abandoned post; defeated by the rain. They headed for their cars or other shelters. The long slow-moving line disintegrated.

He sipped his drink, popped in a handful of M&M's, and felt his semi-new, eight-month-old phone safe in his front pocket. He thought about the $850 he *didn't* spend.

Then he stepped out; just started walking down the sidewalk. In the splashing rain. And he was doing something unique; something nobody else was doing. Not a lemming this time. No stupid line. No chasing the next great thing. And it felt good. And a whimsical smile spread over his face. And he felt the cool water trickle down his back. And he was free. And he liked it.

JOHN LORY

Men For The Ages

He sat there at the mouth of the garage. His eyes were dull and vacant and he feebly stared out into the rainy overcast day that was spread out in front of him. He was positioned at an awkward angle in his wheelchair--sort of leaning to the right--probably because he couldn't hold himself straight. Next to him, in an old lawn chair, was his ever-attentive daughter. She talked to him, but he didn't respond; he couldn't. His vocal cords no longer obeyed his wishes. He was an unwilling mute.

He tried to look at his daughter; the eye muscles refused to cooperate. Life had come full circle. He'd taken care of her when she was young; now she cared for him when he was old, decrepit, and just a shell.

Memories, most of them faded, were locked away, tucked up in his now jumbled and silent mind. He would never share them again.

His legs were useless; he would never walk on them again.

His arms were frozen; he would never use them again.

His hands and fingers were dormant like a statue; no life in them.

It hadn't always been like this. He'd once been strong and stout. An active mind, finely tuned muscles, living a worthy life--a good life. The things he'd experienced. His first job, his first house, the day he got married, the arrival of children, vacations, parties, holidays. His family had looked to him, and he'd kept them safe and sound. The winds of life had blown against him and he'd stood like an oak. And he'd lived, and he'd laughed, and he'd loved, and the picture albums were full of the very best moments of his life.

Now that was gone. It had all dissolved away. Now it was just this wheelchair; a crippled man who had nothing left to give. Alive on the outside; dead on the inside; waiting for the grave.

A couple of older gents, perhaps mid-sixties, stood outside the doors of a restaurant. Ball caps and waterproof, nylon jackets protecting them from the drizzle and the nip of the overcast day. The weather was a minor inconvenience.

And they talked, smiles on their faces. Perhaps it was about the joy of being retired, being able to stand out in front of a restaurant, mid-day, with no deadlines to meet. Perhaps it was about their families--the kids, the grandkids, the wife. Perhaps about that guy they'd both known long ago. Perhaps about nagging arthritis or the new medication the doctor had prescribed.

These men were satisfied, content, happy with life. Much of their lives were in the rearview mirror, but the next day still held promise. The sun would come up and these men would enjoy it with a cup of coffee. Old enough to be in control; young enough to do as they pleased. They walked into the restaurant together. Happy to be in their golden years.

The hood was up on the car and he leaned under it, staring, analyzing, looking for the problem, searching for the offending part. A gray, light-duty sweatshirt covered his 40-year-old frame. The drizzle and bluster of the day did not concern him in the least. What did concern him was the squealing noise that was under the hood. He had to figure it out because he had to work in a couple of hours.

He felt a slight kink and backed out from under the hood. This piece of crap! He was going to buy something new next year. Get something dependable. He could then spend his extra money on a weekend with the family in the Dells instead of on a damn alternator or serpentine belt or whatever failure hid under the hood of this over-the-hill jalopy.

He was beginning to gain traction in life. Things were looking up. His boss liked what he was doing at work. A promotion might be coming down the pike. The wife just got a raise and they were looking toward the future. Move out of the rental, buy their *own* home. Someplace with a backyard where he could toss the football around with his sons. Of course, he'd have to get back into shape--lose that paunch around his waist, dial back on the beers a bit. But he could do it--no problem. He had things to look forward to--aspire to--out on that horizon of life. The things he would do. The things his family would experience. The joys of life were still out there. The memories yet to come.

Now, what to do about this damn car.

They'd always told him smoking was bad, but he didn't care about that.

He stood against the stone wall by the laundromat, a cigarette hung on his lips because, as a twenty-one-year-old, he thought it looked cool.

He glanced up at the gray overcast sky. The gentle drizzle actually felt good on his skinny arms.

Standing in the rain, bare arms, smoking a cigarette--that definitely was cool.

He worked at Dominos, drove car for them, delivering pizzas all over town all hours of the day and night. It was really just minimum wage work, but it provided a paycheck--cold hard cash. He spent it as fast as he earned it. iPhone, wireless Bose headphones, gasoline, other stuff, and of course cigarettes.

They told him he ought to save some of his money. He thought that was stupid. He was young. He'd do boring and responsible stuff when he got older. Right now, however, he was going to have fun. Live life. Tomorrow? Who cared about tomorrow? It was all about today.

There was this girl at work. A saucy spitfire. They liked each other. They joked around--when the boss wasn't looking. She was cool. She was something. He was thinking about asking her out. Would that be weird?

They could hang out. They could do things together. Ride around and listen to their music. Go to movies--stuff like that. Where would it lead? Where *could* it lead?

He wouldn't tell his parents about her. Wouldn't introduce her to them. No friggin way! He didn't need any more old people's advice or scoldings--do this, don't do that. Whatever. He was smart. So was this girl. They could figure out things together *if* she became *his* girl.

He expertly flicked the spent cigarette into a small puddle on the asphalt. His phone buzzed. He fished it out of his back pocket and looked at the screen. It was her! What? She was calling him? A shiver of excitement went through him. Could this phone call be the start of something special?

He'd just arrived home from the hospital a few days ago. He rested in a crisp, new white bassinet, tucked into a onesie that was a bit too big.

His arrival had been met with great joy. According to his glowing parents, he was a marvel; the cutest ever; a gem of the most precious kind. He'd been passed around to adoring relatives. Grandparents, aunts and uncles, close family friends. He'd received a plethora of kisses and snuggles.

And, he *was* special. And he *was* a marvel. For he was a newborn. So helpless, yet so loved. Those tiny feet and toes. Those delicate fingers opening and closing in a gentle rhythm. So small, so insignificant, yet so vital. The future. The next generation.

His parents dreamed of the things he'd do. Dad just knew he'd be a sports star. Maybe football...no maybe soccer...no maybe baseball. Yeah, baseball. He'd be a left-hander. Rocket arm; unhittable. The next Nolan Ryan.

The seventh game of the World Series. Bottom of the ninth. Bases loaded. Nobody out. His team holding a tenuous 1 run lead. They'd call him from the bullpen to save the day. And, he'd deliver. 3 strikeouts. World Champs!

Mom believes he'll become a doctor. Save lives. The one they call when all hope is nearly gone. The magic man. The miracle worker. Skilled hands guided by the very Creator. And with a humble passion, he'd work through the night in the OR, snatching life out of the grip of death. Come out a reluctant hero. And he'd smile for the cameras; say he was just doing his job. And he'd thank his parents for their unwavering support that made him the man he'd become.

But, for now, he rested in the bassinet feeling warm, comfortable, and loved. Cared for by two attentive parents.

And, the next 90 years were waiting out there for him--a road to walk, a story to write.

And, he was completely oblivious to the overcast day and the rain that was pattering against the bedroom window.

A Matter Of Time

Sharon Barber came down the stairs and walked into the kitchen. Sitting at the table, eating a piece of buttered toast, was her daughter, Mattie. A pink beach towel was hanging on the chair behind her.

The patio door curtain was open and the bright morning sun was splashing across the kitchen floor.

"What's the towel for?" Sharon asked her daughter.

"Swimming."

Sharon said nothing but stared through the patio door at the in ground pool twenty-five feet away. Her husband, Tom, had thought that the pool would be a good idea. This coming from a man who also thought buying a set of Ginsu knives out of the back of a magazine was a good idea. This coming from a man who also thought buying a San Diego timeshare was a good idea.

"Family bonding time. Hosting parties. Envy of the neighborhood," Tom had said.

Like that was ever going to happen.

When Tom wasn't working, he was on the golf course or snoring away in his recliner. Sharon didn't even think he had a pair of swimming trunks.

Brad, their nineteen-year-old son, and fourteen-year-old Mattie occasionally used the pool, but mostly it was a pain-in-the-ass maintenance nightmare.

The pool parties Tom had promised they'd host hadn't materialized.

"You can't use the pool today," Sharon finally said. "Dad just took the cover off of it. Water's too cold yet. It won't be at a decent temp for at least a couple of days."

Mattie looked up from her plate of toast. She did not like this tidbit of news.

"But Mom! It's like 80 degrees or something outside. It's almost summer."

"Actually, it's more like 60 outside and it's only early May," Sharon corrected her daughter.

"But..."

"No buts," Sharon said, cutting off Mattie. "No swimming in the pool for a few days."

"Whatever!" Mattie barked, spilling out of her chair and stomping into the living room.

It was amazing how little it took to throw her into a tizzy. The pink towel slid onto the floor.

Sharon shook her head. Teenage girls.

"I'm going to K-Mart," she called out to Mattie, who was now pouting on the couch. "Your dad is out golfing and Brad is at work, so you'll be here alone 'til I get back. Try not to burn the place down, OK?"

Mattie didn't answer.

Sharon stepped out into the attached garage and punched the garage door button. The door growled and creaked as it climbed upward. She slid into her car and turned the key. The thing woofed and chugged a bit before it finally purred to life.

Backing out of the driveway, she sped off to the local K-Mart five miles away.

Saturday morning at K-Mart was a zoo. Sharon patiently and methodically weaved through the crowd with her cart. Big jugs of Hawaiian Punch were on sale. So were giant cellophane bags of popcorn. Sharon picked up one of each.

The line at the pharmacy was enormous. It snaked away from the counter and into the main aisle of the store. Sharon decided she'd skip getting the Anacin--maybe next time.

It took forever and a day to get through the checkout. Two check out aisles open; twelve closed; cashiers as motivated as a well-fed hog in a mud hole in mid-June. She lugged her purchases out to the car and struggled to get the key into the trunk keyhole. Mercifully, the trunk finally popped open and with great relief, Sharon dumped the bags into the wide-open expanse. Curiously, the trunk light did not come on.

She opened the driver's door. The dome light did not come on. Behind the wheel, Sharon turned the key. Click, click, click, click,

click. Odd. She tried again. More rapid clicking. The car was not starting.

Sharon was at a loss as to what to do. She didn't know very much about cars. What was wrong? Why didn't it start? She felt a twinge of anxiety begin to grow and she quickly went through her options. Try to open the hood? Try to call Tom or Brad? Try to call an auto repair shop?

She decided to start by opening the hood; see if something looked amiss underneath. Having watched Tom open the hood numerous times, she pulled the lever inside and then made her way outside. She fumbled with the latch under the hood for a few minutes before she figured out how it worked. Sharon gawked inside. Hoses, wires, bolts, nuts, fan blades, other metal thingys. She might as well be looking at a quantum physics equation--it was all foreign to her.

"You having problems, ma'am?"

Sharon whirled around with a start. She felt red embarrassment spread down her face.

"Sorry, didn't mean to startle you," the older man said. "Just wondering if you're having problems with your car."

The man was stubby with bifocals and a mop of heavy gray hair parted on the side. His face was slightly pocked and he had a whiskey nose. His smile was kind.

"It just won't start," Sharon said, shrugging.

"Well, perhaps today is your lucky day," the fellow said. "Name's Fred, been a certified auto mechanic for the last twenty-five years. You want me to take a look?

It felt like a giant sack of concrete had just been lifted off of her shoulders.

"Well, if you wouldn't mind, I'd appreciate it."

"Let's see what we've got here," Fred said, ducking under the hood. "You say it doesn't start?"

Sharon nodded.

"Slide inside and turn the key once," Fred told her. "Let's see how it sounds."

Sharon got in the car. She turned the key. Click, click, click....

Fred backed out from under the hood.

"Try your headlights now."

Sharon pulled the knob and watched as Fred looked down and nodded.

"Okay, ma'am you can shut them off."

Sharon complied.

"Looks like you've got a dead battery," Fred told her.

"Is that bad?" Sharon quizzed him, as she climbed out of the car.

"Oh, it's more of a hassle than anything," Fred chuckled. "Nothing to get too worked up about, all things considered."

"What should I do?"

"Well, tell you what. If you don't mind waiting a few minutes, I can give you a jump."

"A jump?"

"Yeah, pretty simple," Fred said. "I'll bring my car over, hook my good battery to your dead one and that'll get your car started and get you home. Then you can buy a new battery and your problem will be solved."

"That is great," Sharon replied, thinking how nice it would be to just get home and let Tom worry about the car.

"Tell you what," Fred continued. "I've got to drop a prescription off at the pharmacy--before the darn thing closes for the day-- then I can give you a jump. Should be only a few minutes, if you don't mind."

"No, that's great."

"OK, I'll be right back."

Sharon watched as Fred turned and headed for the store at a slow shuffling plod. She took a deep sigh and leaned up against her car. What a lucky break! A certified auto mechanic shows up at just the perfect time. Couldn't have written it better.

As she waited for Fred to return, she looked up into the sky. Rolling gray clouds had replaced the bright sun and it looked like it might rain. Hopefully, Fred would get her on the road before that happened.

She watched the traffic exiting the store.

When she saw the guy, her nose automatically wrinkled up. He was an example of what was wrong with the current generation.

28

Skinny as a rail, dirty black tank top with AC/DC plastered across it. Ripped jeans. Heart tattoo on the left bicep. Long stringy hair down to the middle of his back, mirror shades, thin goatee, and a silver earring dangling off his left lobe.

She thought about Mattie for a moment. Please, God, don't let Mattie come home with a guy like that.

*Hey, mom, let me introduce you to my new boyfriend...*She shuddered.

With utter disdain, she watched as the *guy* loped towards her carrying a box of car speakers under his arm. As he got closer, she turned away so there was no chance they'd make eye contact. The loser walked by, and Sharon breathed a sigh of relief that he was gone.

Shortly, Sharon heard a loud rumble followed by the deep thump of bass music. She looked down at the end of the parking lot. How typical. It was the hooligan. He'd climbed into this loud red beast, brought it to life, and turned the volume on his stereo up to ten.

She watched; listened. Thump, thump, thump of the bass. He revved the motor sending a cloud of icky exhaust up into the air.

Sharon rolled her eyes in disgust.

The hooligan shifted the car and tore out of his parking spot. As he roared down the row, she turned away and pretended to be looking into her car. Soon he would be gone.

She was understandably confused then, when he didn't blow past her, but pulled into the parking spot in front of her and skidded to an abrupt stop; the front of his car inches away from her's.

Sharon's heart began to pound wildly. What was going on now? She managed a discreet look out of the corner of her eye. His car was a red Pontiac Trans-Am with a giant, gaudy red firebird stamped across the hood. A big black hood scoop sat between the ghastly firebird's wings, the music continued to thump, and noxious smelling exhaust billowed out of the monstrous rumbling car. Then the noise stopped. The guy shut off the engine--the thumping music dying with it.

Sharon looked into the driver's side window of her car, debating whether or not to get inside and manually lock the door. Why did this lowlife stop? Why did he park right in front of her? Was he going to rob her? Her purse was sitting in the front passenger seat.

She looked up when she heard the heavy door of the Trans-Am thud shut. The skinny guy was right there. He was looking at her. She felt uneasy.

"Having car trouble?" he asked.

Sharon looked at him closer. He seemed quiet and more soft-spoken than she'd imagined. He had sort of a smile on his face.

"Uh, just a dead battery," she managed.

"Want a jump?" he asked.

"Naw," she quickly responded, looking towards the front of the store. "I've got a friend inside who's going to help me...thanks anyway."

"You sure?" he asked. "It'd only take a minute. It wouldn't be a problem."

She let his statement hang in mid-air as she continued to stare at the exit doors of K-Mart. Where was Fred? When was he going to come out?

She sighed, confused about what to do. Awkward. Desperate. Finally, she turned towards the waiting kid. She wanted to tell him to go away; get lost; just leave her alone. Didn't she say she had it under control? But, she couldn't bring herself to be rude or unappreciative.

"Yeah, sure, I guess. Go ahead if you don't mind."

This seemed to please the kid. He smiled. In a flash, he dug a pair of jumper cables out of his backseat. Like an expert, he quickly hooked them up.

"You wanna get in your car and get ready to turn the key?"

She nodded, and the skinny kid leaped into the big red Trans-Am. Seconds later the brutish car was alive again. The music began to thump. Sharon waited as the kid revved the car a few times. Then he was back out next to her car. He gave her a thumbs-up sign.

"Give it a shot."

Not optimistic, Sharon tentatively turned the key. Presto! Her car came to life. While she was taking a moment to compose herself, the guy disconnected the cables, slammed the hood of the Trans-Am, and gently but firmly closed her hood.

"You're all ready to go now," he said.

Before she had a chance to do or say anything, he was back in his car. His tires squawked as he backed out of the parking spot. He screeched to a stop. Shifting into drive, he spun the tires slightly,

31

rocketed down to the end of the row, and flew across the parking lot towards the exit as if he'd been shot out of a cannon.

Sharon managed to get out of her car and watched and listened as the roaring red Trans-Am disappeared down the road; the loud engine and thumping music drifting into oblivion.

She was left standing next to her car amid the quiet methodical humming of her engine. How strange, she thought. She shook her head and got back into her car. She sat behind the wheel. What should she do now? Should she wait for Fred? Again she looked up at the K-Mart exit doors. She remembered how busy the pharmacy had been when she was inside. Fred could be awhile. She tapped on the wheel. She didn't imagine Fred would mind if he came out and she was gone. Yeah, she'd just head home.

It was drizzling and the day had cooled quite a bit by the time Sharon arrived home. She hit the remote and waited as the garage door chugged upward. She pulled in, shut off the car, and retrieved her bags from the trunk.

"Mattie, I'm home!" she called out as she came in the front door.

No answer.

She walked into the kitchen and looked out the patio door. Then she saw it. It was Mattie, in the pool. But, something didn't look right. Mattie was just bobbing up and down, awkwardly floating, like she was a ragdoll, her face barely above water. Fear and motherly instinct kicked in. This wasn't right. Without a moment's hesitation, she dropped her packages. The big jug of red Hawaiian Punch bounced once when it hit the floor and then ruptured. Red liquid splashed all over the place. Sharon stepped on the cellophane bag of popcorn as she made a mad dash for the pool. The bag burst with a loud *poof* and popcorn fluttered through the air.

"Mattie, Mattie!" Sharon screamed as she skidded to a stop at the edge of the pool. There was no acknowledgment. Mattie's skin had a sickly blue hue to it and one of her hands was weakly hanging onto the edge of the concrete pool.

Sharon lunged forward and coarsely grabbed Mattie's arm; she managed to drag her daughter out of the pool. The girl was cold and lifeless.

"Mattie! Mattie! Are you OK? Wake up, wake up, oh God!"

Nothing.

Tears welling up, Sharon raced back to the kitchen. She sloshed through the punch and popcorn, grabbed the phone, and called 9-1-1. She hysterically explained the situation, gave the address, and raced back to Mattie leaving the dispatcher still on the line.

Sharon shook Mattie gently, pleaded with her to move, wiggle a finger or toe.

She was only vaguely aware of the sheriff's deputy who arrived on the scene. In a daze, she watched as the deputy began to perform CPR.

Moments later, an ambulance screamed into the driveway.

They raced Mattie Barber to the hospital.

They said she almost didn't make it. They said she almost didn't come back. They said her survival had come down to a matter of minutes.

They said that if Sharon had not arrived home when she did, Mattie Barber would have died.

Now, Sharon sat in the hospital room watching her little girl's chest gently rising and falling. It was evening, the time of the day when all things inevitably begin to settle. And, Sharon wanted to enjoy the quiet, but her mind wouldn't let her. For the loud rumbling of a red Trans-Am and the pounding pulse of a deep bass beat resonated in her head. The smell of soggy air saturated with thick, hot exhaust was still stuck in her nostrils, and in her mind's eye stood a skinny, reckless looking kid--a kid who had ended up being the biggest hero her world had ever known.

Spirit Of '73

Maybe my name is Millie.

Maybe I've got raven hair that is shiny and smooth, and maybe it's tied up in a couple of uneven pigtails that bounce when I walk.

Maybe I'm wearing this little, frilly, white blouse that hangs to my waist, a pair of jean capris, white ankle socks, and the cutest pair of little sneakers that you ever did see.

Maybe I've got my own room with walls of pink.

Over there is my bed and my teddy bear. Teddy sits on my pillow all day. He's worn out and ratty, but I sleep with him every night and I love him.

Right over there, under the window, is where I'll have a sturdy wooden desk one day. It's where I'll sit and do my homework; it's where I'll write that essay that gets an A+ and gets read up in front of the class.

Across the room, up against the far wall, is a little white dresser. It's fine for now, but one day I'll get a bigger one with a large mirror. A brush and comb will sit on top of it along with that little plastic penguin I got from Sea World, crumpled notes from my school friends, and the red and gold trophy I won at the dance studio.

I'll have posters on the walls. Cartoon characters for starters, then my favorite movies or TV shows, then scenic landscapes; the mountains of Colorado; a sunset over a sparkling lake.

Maybe I'm outside now. I think that's where I like it best.

That's the driveway over there. It's where I'll learn to drive a tricycle, then a bicycle, then a car.

That's the yard out that way. I love being in the yard. Those days of bright sun, blue skies, and a carpet of thick-headed, yellow dandelions. I'll pick myself a bouquet. I won't notice the grass stains on my knees.

Maybe they say my smile lights up a room when I walk in. I know it's cliché but it still could be true. I plan on making my mark on this world.

Maybe there is going to be a file of pictures--a virtual photo album that records my life. There's one when I came home from the hospital as a newborn; there's one from the first day of kindergarten. There's one from the prom. My wedding day. Birthdays, vacations, other special events. They are all there. My imprint on the world. My life.

Maybe I will make a difference out there. Not that I'll be rich or famous or invent something amazing, but I can be a friend. I can care.

Maybe I have a family.

Maybe I am loved.

Maybe I'm special.

Or maybe not.

It is a cruel and ruthless world and, unfortunately, I was one of the unlucky ones.

Maybe I never had a choice.

Maybe I never had a chance.

So, sadly, no one knows my name. For I am just a ghost, unwanted, forgotten; destined to roam in the shadows of darkness. For I didn't matter; my time was short; I was just a breathless whisper in a roaring hurricane.

But thankfully, my pain did not endure. In the end, I was not forgotten. For Love found me and took me by the hand. And now I walk in endless fields of gold, underneath a pure sky of sparkling diamonds.

 And I dance among the angels beneath the vibrant glow of the eternal light.

JOHN LORY

The Disappearance Of David Conroy

David Conroy disappeared yesterday and nobody knows why.

I know this because I worked with David Conroy. Like me, he was a data entry clerk and his cubicle was next to mine.

I just know I'm going to get called in and asked about him. I'll go mostly because I don't have a choice, but what will I tell them? I didn't know that much about David. He was just a data entry clerk whose cubicle was next to mine.

Now, normally having somebody miss a day of work isn't a big deal. People get sick. People have doctor's appointments and vacation days. But this was different. David Conroy didn't miss work. He came in every day on time and in my humble opinion did an excellent job.

We'd have a few casual conversations from time-to-time. How about that weather? What are you doing this weekend? Did they change brands of coffee in the breakroom?

I'd say he was a nice guy, genuine, good listener. He had a way of remembering something you told him and he'd ask about it later. So, your wife getting over her cough? Your daughter get that new car? How'd your flower planting go over the weekend? Like your new grill?

Personally, I liked him for that. The world is chock full of blowhards and self-absorbed egotists. Nobody listens--they just bloviate about themselves, but that wasn't David Conroy.

It was kind of weird to see David's cubicle dark and deserted. It got even weirder when Dixie came clomping down the hallway in her hoof-like shoes. She went into David's workstation and rooted around in his stuff like an old sow looking for a hidden ear of corn.

Dixie is our supervisor. She's tall, needle-thin, and she plasters her eyes with blue eyeliner. Remember the stuff I said about the world being chock full of blowhards? Well, Dixie is a card-carrying member of that group. Most of our pod's weekly meetings are taken up by Dixie and her all-about-me stories. She's done everything you have and more. Got a medical ailment? She's already had it and it was much worse than your case. If I'm correct she's had brain surgery, broken nose, kidney stones, gout, stomach stapling, stricture, irritable bowel syndrome, arthritis, temporary blindness, hysterectomy, alcohol dependency, cataracts, female pattern baldness, hip, shoulder, and knee replacements, 24 hours of hiccups, ringworm, panic attacks, root canal, and has been struck by lightning twice.

She's an expert on politics, road trips, parasailing, auto mechanics, home heating and cooling systems, painting, astronomy, drywalling, vitamins, fine dining, liquor, interior decorating, 3D printing, inter-office networking, knitting, shoe repair, movies, mechanical bulls and dump trucks--and that's not an all-inclusive list.

Except for a few ass kissers in our pod, nobody can stand Dixie. Most would rather avoid her at all costs.

Anyway, whatever Dixie was looking for in David's cubicle, she didn't find it. I saw her tromp back to her office with a scowl on her face.

Ned Brewster, the data entry clerk across the hall, snuck into my cube after Dixie left.

"What's going on?" he hoarsely whispered with his nasty coffee breath.

"I don't know," I shrugged. "David didn't come in today."

"Shit," Ned said nervously, his little eyes ferreting about. "Think he got sent away?"

"Dunno," I shrugged. "But I betcha Dixie will be back soon looking for something."

The possibility of Dixie appearing caused Ned to scurry back to his cube.

I didn't want to speculate on what was going on and I most certainly didn't want to think about David Conroy getting sent away to a reeducation camp.

The next morning my cubicle phone rang. I picked it up. It was Dixie.

"Please come to my office directly," she blared. "We've got some questions for you."

I put down the receiver, leaned back in my chair, and took a deep breath. Yep, this was what I was fearing. The questioning.

I made my way past all the little gray cubicles to Dixie's office. I knocked and entered her domain. She and a guy in black suit and tie were sitting at a round conference table in one corner of the office.

"Have a seat," Dixie said, pointing to an open chair.

I sat down and gave the dude in the suit a once over. He was a pale, sickly-looking fellow with a long somber face, big ears, and bushy eyebrows. His black hair was pasted back against his skull revealing a number of forehead wrinkles. He looked about as friendly as a rabid dog. I nodded at him. He didn't move.

"Well, Jack, this man is Morton Gould, he's from ACT and he'd like to ask you some questions."

ACT--a new government agency that was specifically created, in my opinion, to control the masses. ACT stood for Acceptance, Compliance, and Tolerance. It'd been the brainchild of some ultra-progressive visionaries who were convinced the system set up by the Founding Fathers was flawed.

The ACT folks felt they could do things better.

It took about fifteen years for the liberal ACT caucus to get a foothold into the government. But, like an oozing river of slime, they eventually leaked in and set up shop. They instituted changes to make us a "more perfect union". Those who resisted or disagreed with ACT were either sent to reeducation camps or simply disappeared. ACT had a lot in common with the Nazi's

Morton Gould gave me a disapproving stare and opened a leather-bound notebook. He placed it in front of himself and cleared his throat.

"Name, please?" he said in a dry monotone croak.

42

I looked at Dixie. She gave me a condescending nod.

"Uh, Jack. Jack Dray," I said.

Morton scrawled my name in his notebook and then looked at me.

"Now, Mr. Dray, what we are conducting here is an official and confidential government-sanctioned interview. You will be under the ACT oath and required to tell the truth. The contents of our interview are to remain confidential. You are to share nothing that transpires in this official interview under penalty of law. Do you understand?"

I shrugged, "Yeah, sure."

"Very well," Morton Gould said, sliding his chair back a few inches. "Now, what do you know about David Conroy?"

I was quiet for a moment, my mind spinning. What did I know about David Conroy? How was I supposed to answer that?

"Um, I'm not sure what you mean," I hedged.

Morton was not impressed, "Do you know David Conroy?"

I nodded.

"Tell us what you know."

"Uh, well, we work side-by-side in data entry," I began. "He seems like a good guy and we chit chat now and then....I think he's got a wife and a son...that's about all I know."

"Do you know of his whereabouts?" Morton asked.

"Huh? Whereabouts? What do you mean?"

"He's gone," Dixie butted in. "Do you know where he is?"

"No, I don't," I replied, wrinkling my brow. "Why do you ask?"

"That doesn't matter," Morton Gould cut in. "So, you're saying you have no knowledge of his current location, then?"

"That's what I'm saying," I snapped back.

"And are you, under penalty of law, telling us the truth today?"

I *so* wanted to reply to that with some witty, sarcastic retort.

"Yes, I am," I opted to reply.

"Did David Conroy ever talk about anything you'd consider inappropriate under the ACT charter?" Mr. Gould asked dryly.

"Like what?" I asked, genuinely confused.

"Like anything that's illegal to talk about," Dixie rudely cut in again.

"We talked about the weather, the coffee in the breakroom, and stuff like that. Like I said, just chit chat. It's not like we were buddies outside of work or anything...what the heck is this about anyway?"

"Just answer the questions," Morton drawled as he wrote more things in his little notebook.

"No, he never talked about anything inappropriate."

"You sure?" Dixie asked, a hint of accusation in her voice.

"No, nothing." I shot back, feeling my ire rise.

"OK, Mr. Dray," Morton said, looking down at his page of notes. "Thank you for your time...and remember this interview is to remain confidential. Understand?"

I got to my feet and nodded. I walked out of Dixie's office feeling as if I was exiting the stuffy confines of a sauna. What the hell was that all about?

When I got back to my cube, Ned Brewster was waiting.

"So, what were you doing in Dixie's office? What happened? What's going on? Was it about David?"

"Nah," I said, sitting down in my cubicle chair. "Just work stuff. Nothing important.

Ned seemed disappointed by this. He quietly sulked back to his workstation.

Moments later, I heard Ned's phone chirp. After a brief, muted conversation, I watched him head towards Dixie's office. Guess he'd soon find out the real reason I met with demanding Dixie.

Suddenly, I didn't feel like working, but since the place was inundated with video cameras, I turned my attention to the computer screen. I absently poked on the keyboard, but my thoughts were elsewhere.

What was the deal with David Conroy? Why was he missing? Why were people being called into Dixie's office to be interviewed by a guy who reminded me of a wild west undertaker? What weren't these ACT bastards telling us this time?

Ned Brewster returned to his cube about fifteen minutes later. He was oddly quiet and I saw nothing of him for the rest of the day. At quitting time, while I was getting my sweatshirt and surrounded by fellow workers, Ned bumped me on the shoulder. When I looked over at him, he pretended not to notice me.

"Meet me at Shell Park, fifteen minutes," he muttered quickly, not looking in my direction.

I said nothing, gathered my sweatshirt, and headed for the front doors. Outside in my car, I sat behind the wheel and thought about Ned Brewster. What was he up to and why did he want to meet at Shell Park?

I thought about not going. However, I felt curiosity tugging at me. Besides, if I stood him up today he'd be badgering me non-stop for the rest of the week. Starting my car, I headed over to Shell Park.

Despite there being a number of cars in the park's lot, I spotted Ned's lime green Toyota. I pulled into a slot and got out.

It was actually a nice day. Sunny with a few clouds; a small breeze. I walked across the asphalt lot and into the park, following a cobblestone path. There were a few kids hanging on the monkey bars; there was a young couple sitting together on one of the many green picnic tables. An old lady was walking one of those nasty little furry dogs across a wide expanse of green lawn; cheering was coming from the ball field across the street, but where the heck was Ned?

I continued on the cobblestone path, following it down a small rise to the riverwalk. There I spotted Ned standing down by the bubbling stream, under a low hanging crab apple tree, tossing small pebbles into the water.

He heard me coming and looked up.

"What's up, Ned?" I asked as I walked closer.

He dumped his handful of pebbles on the ground, wiped his hand down his pants leg, and nervously looked around.

"What's going on, Jack?"

"What do you mean?" I asked.

"At work; David Conroy. What's going on? You had a talk with that guy in Dixie's office, right?"

I nodded.

"So why are they dragging us in under ACT for interviews? What's going on? Why are they asking all these questions about David? What are they getting at? Are they trying to get us in trouble? Implicate us in something? Are they gonna haul us off to the camps?"

Ned was in a nervous tizzy. I held up my hand.

"Slow down a minute," I said. "I don't know what's going on, but obviously David is missing and for some reason, it's bothering them."

"What happened in Dixie's office? Did that big dope ask you a bunch of questions?"

"He wanted to know what I knew about David," I said. "I told him what little information I had about the guy."

"That's all?"

"Yeah. Why? What did they ask you?" I quizzed.

"Same stuff as you, I guess," Ned said, seeming to calm a bit. "The guy asked me if David ever talked about inappropriate stuff."

"Yeah, same here," I replied. "What did you say?"

"Nothing really...then I remembered once when David talked to me about his religion...I told them about that time."

"His religion?"

"Yeah, one time he said something about God or Jesus--something like that. I don't remember exactly."

"Well, you know how ACT hates religion," I said. "Unsanctioned religious activities would be a violation of ACT."

"Well, you know what I think happened?" Ned cut me off. "I think David was doing illegal stuff with his religion. I think he got caught and sent to one of those reeducation camps or whatever. I had a neighbor who said his cousin or somebody got in trouble for doing that...sent him to some work camp...never was heard from again."

I thought about that for a moment, "If David got sent to a camp by ACT then why are they asking us if we know where he's at? Doesn't make any sense."

"Because it's a cover," Ned bristled. "They're pretending they don't know anything, then they bring us in and question us and try to find out if we've been doing something wrong too so they can ship us off to a work camp. Those jerks."

"Maybe," I shrugged. "If they're looking for anything on me then they're going to be majorly disappointed. I go to work; I go home. I follow the rules, pay my taxes, and don't mess with religion or anything that ACT has outlawed."

"Well, I don't like it," Ned growled.

"Don't worry. If you haven't done anything wrong then you got nothing to worry about, right?"

"I guess," Ned said.

"Well, I gotta get home," I told him, looking around. "I'll see you at work tomorrow, OK?"

I left Ned by the riverwalk and went home.

That night, I had trouble sleeping. I kept thinking about David Conroy, my interview, and Ned Brewster's conspiracy theories. I tried to remember more about David Conroy. I went over the conversations I had with him in the past. Did he say anything inappropriate? Anything against ACT regulations? Not that I could remember.

However, religion and whatnot was a definite violation of the government ACT charter. Religion was one of the first things ACT outlawed when they gained power. People could still go to church if they wanted, but they needed to keep what they learned and talked about to themselves and not spout it off outside the church. ACT said it was the separation of church and state or whatever. They said church-speak outside the church building violated Acceptance and Tolerance statutes.

Me, I didn't see the big deal. If the government lets you go to church, then go there and do your talking or Jesus worship or singing in the building and in the privacy of your home. Why try and force it on other people who didn't want to hear it? Not that I had anything against religion. My grandma was very religious. She went to church every Sunday. I even went to the church sometimes on Christmas Eve and Easter and I was generally a good person.

Thing is, though, something still bugged me about the whole David Conroy issue. What happened to him? Where was he, and why was I being asked about it? Maybe there was more to the story. Maybe I should do some snooping around.

I'm not a detective, but I knew Dixie was messing around in David's cube a couple of days ago. Maybe there was something worth knowing in David's workspace. Getting into David's cubicle to look around would be fairly easy.

The following morning I stopped in Dixie's office. She looked up from a stack of papers when I came in.

"Yes?" She said, making it apparent that I was disturbing her massively important work.

"Uh, yeah, um, last week David Conroy was supposed to give me those data entry summaries...obviously, he's not here, but I figured since you're the boss and in charge of everything you probably know where they're at."

A big smile spread over Dixie's normally dour face. She loved the fact that she was the boss. Now that I stroked her ego, I wasn't such a bother.

"He did not give them to me," she said. "However, they might be in his cubicle. Why don't you just go in there and see if you can find them."

Arrogant people. They are so easy to manipulate.

"OK, I just wanted to make sure I had your permission to go into somebody else's cube."

"You have my permission," she beamed.

Arrogant people. They are so easy to manipulate.

I walked into David's cubicle, turned on his light, and looked around.

Not much to see. I looked over some work papers on the desk. I found the data summary reports right on the top but I continued my search.

Moving my back to strategically block the video camera sticking in the corner of the big pod room, I opened the two drawers on the left side of his desk. The top drawer had nothing important in it-- just some work folders, an employee manual, and a bottle of ibuprofen. There was more of the same in the second drawer. I was about to close it up and move on when my eye caught something at the very bottom of the drawer. Careful that I was obscuring the video camera, I lifted up a ream of paper, and underneath it was a small hardcover book. It had a cross on the front cover and the title was The Perfect Sinner's Devotion Book. I picked it up and sifted through it. Page after page of bible verses and such--religious stuff--that was a clear violation of the ACT statutes. As I stared at the little book, I began to feel queasy. Here I was in possession of outlawed religious material! I quickly pushed the book back under the paper ream, dropped a pile of folders on top, and closed the drawer.

I grabbed the data entry summaries and left David's cube. Back at my own workstation, I spread out the data summary reports and pretended to look them over. In truth, the stuff was the furthest thing from my mind.

David Conroy was a lawbreaker according to the government. He was in possession of banned religious material. Personally, I couldn't care less if David had a devotion book at work and I thought it was a stupid reason to send somebody to a reeducation camp. Of course, it was also stupid for somebody to bring something like that to work. Why didn't he just leave the thing at home?

However, this still didn't clear up the mystery of his disappearance. I came back to my earlier questions. If ACT caught David with unlawful literature and sent him to a camp, why were they questioning his co-workers?

Ned seemed to think they were trying to set a trap for possible co-conspirators but I didn't buy that for one minute.

David Conroy was missing and nobody, including the big shots at ACT, knew where he was. Not knowing something; not having control of somebody--that was what was bugging ACT, and in my estimation, that was what they were trying to remedy.

I didn't know why I cared about the situation. My interview had pretty much summed up my involvement with David Conroy and I certainly didn't want to run afoul the law. My life was pretty good as is. Sure, if I had my way, some things would change, but all in all, I had few complaints. If ACT wanted to run the government, set policy, and deal with the problems it was fine by me as long as I had what I needed. Religion--I really didn't need that so whether or not we could go to church or read bible passages out of a tiny book was of little concern to me.

Still, I was curious as to what happened to David.

I knew where David lived, and so when I got off work, I cruised out into his neighborhood. I slowly drove by his brick ranch house.

Metal stakes had been put up around the perimeter of the home, and yellow tape with ACT INVESTIGATION printed on it was hanging from the stakes. Hmmm, David Conroy's house was a crime scene?

What about his wife and kid? Did they disappear with David? Or, did David do something crazy like kill his wife and kid and then take off somewhere? Not likely. David seemed the furthest thing from a cold-blooded killer I'd ever seen.

Driving back home, my mind was spinning. Why was David's house a crime scene? What was going on in there? Then I got a crazy idea: I could sneak inside and see.

That night, shortly before midnight, I left my apartment. As I drove to David's neighborhood, I felt kinda like I was a secret agent. In the back of my mind, I knew there was always a chance I could get caught trespassing in an ACT crime scene. Couple that with the fact that I knew David Conroy, and I could be in some really deep trouble. But, for some reason, I needed to know what had happened to him.

A couple of blocks from David's house was a 24-hour Wal-Mart. I parked in the lot and started towards my destination on foot. It was a warm humid night and as I got further away from Wal-Mart the quieter it became. Most of the houses on the streets were dark, the inhabitants probably sound asleep inside. I did not encounter as much as a barking dog as I made my way to David's.

When I got to the beginning of David's street, I stopped, bent down, and pretended to tie my shoe. Actually, I was discreetly scanning the area for any obtrusive video cameras with their little blinking red lights. The area seemed clear, so I quickly stood up and made my way to David Conroy's house. With a quick glance over my shoulder, I ducked under the ACT tape and crept into the backyard.

David's backyard was dark, but I could still see the silhouette of the house looming in front of me. I crept up to the back access door into the garage. I tried the knob. It was locked. I stopped and took a deep breath. Perhaps the patio door?

I climbed up onto the deck and tugged on the sliding door. I was expecting it to be locked, but to my surprise, it slid open. I weaseled into the house and battled my way through a thick auburn colored patio curtain. I stopped and stood still, listening.

The home was quiet. In the dim light, I saw I was in a dining room. A wooden table with four chairs surrounding it was placed squarely in the middle of the room under a small chandelier. A vase of wilted flowers sat in the center of the table. To the left of me was a breakfast bar with two barstools and behind that was the kitchen. I pulled out my phone and turned on the flashlight, setting the brightness to the lowest level. Careful to shield the light, I walked forward into a living room. Carpeted floor, a couple of recliners, a couch, a flatscreen TV on a stand. To my right was a hallway. I walked down it. A couple of bedrooms, the bathroom, a closet at the end. I opened the closet and shined my light inside. Coats were hung neatly on hangers, shoes and boots lined up beneath them on a rubber mat. I was shutting the closet when I heard the wailing of a police siren. My heart jumped into my throat. I cut the light and stood still. The siren grew closer and I panicked. I hurried back down the hallway and into the dining room. I saw flashing blue and red lights growing closer through the patio curtain. Moments later, a police car screamed past the house and the siren noise slowly faded. I breathed a sigh of relief and looked around. What was I doing here? I'd put myself in potential danger and found nothing that would bring any clarity to the situation.

I slipped out of the patio door and stood on the deck, no closer to learning the fate of my co-worker. I guessed it was time to forget this silly fascination with David Conroy and get on with life.

I noticed that the air had cooled quite a bit since I'd entered the house. A chilly breeze fluttered through the backyard, cutting into the humid evening and causing goosebumps to perk on my forearms. I shuddered slightly and rubbed my hands together. Just then there was the sound of violent thunder galloping across the sky, quickly followed by a string of wicked purple lightning that ripped across the night, momentarily revealing a bank of ominous thunderheads out on the horizon. It looked to me like a wild storm was coming. I hopped off of David Conroy's deck and started out at a measured jog, aiming to get back to my car before anarchy erupted from the heavens above.

JOHN LORY

All Gone

It was one of those console TV's that was in fashion back in the day. A behemoth with a host of round dials and sliding buttons on the front of it. The thing sat, unmovable, under the large picture window in my grandparent's living room. This was back before the sleek, flat-screen, throw-away TV's with remote controls graced nearly the entire wall of the average person's home. This console TV was a part of the living room decor, a coordinated piece of furniture; it had a couple of potted plants sitting on top of it. This TV was valuable; sort of a status symbol. If it quit working it was taken to the TV repair shop to be fixed.

I loved this TV because it brought me the world, in all its splendid colors, every Sunday afternoon. Professional wrestling, NFL Football, Major League Baseball, Walter Cronkite, the Disney Sunday Movie.

It was a mid-seventies, red Ford pickup with a silver topper. It belonged to my grandpa. He had it parked in his neat, two-car garage and he washed and waxed it religiously. It sparkled. It had this smell; sort of a rubbery/dusty/earthy aroma.

I loved this truck because I got to go places with grandpa. I'd go to the Piggly Wiggly with him to pick up chicken legs, bacon, brand name potato chips, and Jolly Good soda. He'd let me walk down the Pig's gleaming aisle full of candy. He'd pick up a box or two of Chiclets gum and let me pick up a large Nestle Crunch bar, providing I promised to share it with my four sisters.

We'd drive the truck down to the old bridge out on Mitchell Hollow Road so his dog, Bogger, could stretch his legs and chase butterflies. The windows would be down and Grandpa would drive with his right wrist resting on the top of the steering wheel and his left elbow hanging out his window.

He had an odd habit of catcalling random kids who were out playing on the sidewalks. He'd lean out of the window as we rolled by and bark out "Get out of the street!" It would startle the kids and he'd look over at me with a smile. I would laugh.

It was a pump-action Daisy BB gun. My grandpa kept it mounted on two nails on the bulkhead of the basement steps. If I stood on the very edge of my tiptoes, while on the second step, I could reach the thing.

I loved this little gun and when nobody was paying attention, I'd bring it down and take it out into the back yard. There, I would set up a couple of aluminum cans at the base of a giant maple. Pumping the gun to life, I'd become Clint Eastwood in The Good, The Bad, And The Ugly, dropping the bad guys like they were mosquitoes at a nighttime campfire. The BB's would harmlessly plink off of the cans or the tree. I was careful with my aim, fearful that a wayward shot might take out one of the neighbor's windows. Unbeknownst to me, the light-duty gun couldn't launch a BB far enough to reach the neighbor's house.

When I was done, I'd stand on my tiptoes and put the gun away. It'd be there the next time Blondie needed a hand.

These things were part of my life. And, as a kid, I did not think about a time when they would disappear. There would always be another Sunday in front of the console TV. The red Ford would last forever; so would Grandpa; so would his dog, Bogger. There would always be trips to Piggly Wiggly and Chiclets and Nestle Crunch bars. The Daisy would always be perched above the stairs waiting for me, and I'd always have to stand on my tiptoes to reach it.

Oh, the pure naivety of youth!

The first thing to change was Bogger. The old dog passed away one night; my grandpa didn't get a replacement.

The next thing to change was me. I grew up. My interests shifted. I had better things to do on Sunday afternoon than sit in front of a console TV. I got my own car and the red Ford no longer held its appeal. Piggly Wiggly quickly lost its allure; I could now buy my own gum and candy, and I was no longer interested in being a gunslinger with a pump Daisy.

I didn't think about time. Tomorrow was just another day in a long line of days and weeks and months and years to come. There was always something new out on the horizon for me.

I wonder if my grandpa thought about time? Probably. Did he miss his grandson coming around? Probably. Did he see the bulk of his life in the past? Probably.

Grandpa's health went south. He was in and out of the nursing home and hospital. He lost the spark he once had. He died at the age of 79. I was 24.

My grandma remained. She had the console TV for a few years 'til it became too old, outdated, and inoperable. Nobody fixed TV's anymore anyway. One day, it was gone.

I saw the red Ford one last time when my brother-in-law bought it for a few hundred bucks. The bright sheen was gone. The wheel wells were caked with a cancer of rust bubbles. One of the hubcaps was missing. The tires were bald--the white walls covered with road grime. The motor and transmission were shot. In a couple of years, it was in a junkyard.

Then, grandma died and the house was cleaned out and readied for sale.

Two nails remained in the bulkhead, but the BB gun was gone. I never saw it again.

Once in a great while, when I'm back home, I will drive up into my grandparent's old neighborhood. The house is still there; the same color as it always was, but it holds another family. If the walls of that house could talk, they'd have memories to share and stories to tell. But walls don't talk--they just age.

All vestiges of my grandparents are nearly gone. Their tombstones stand out in a small country cemetery, but there remains little in this world to even prove they existed. Perhaps there are a few pictures, maybe a few reminiscent stories told by old people; perhaps a tiny shred of something somebody thought to write down.

But Master Time is not yet done with my grandparents. One day, the pictures will be lost or hidden. The old storytellers themselves will die. Nobody will read the ramblings of some fool. The tombstones will become weathered and ancient, hovering over the forgotten. Then my grandparents will be just names. Then time will be done with them.

It rumbles on another day, the hands of time they will not stay.
And it rumbles on, and it rumbles on, and it rumbles on...

JOHN LORY

Smart Josef

I'm way smarter than everybody else and that's my problem.

My name is Josef Durmaz. I'm only twelve years old, but strangely, I'm a high school sophomore. It's because I'm smart. They say my intelligence comes from my parents. My father is a language professor; my mother is a doctor. They uprooted me from my home country of Turkey and brought me to the United States because they saw it as an opportunity. We settled in some exclusively white, small town in the Midwest.

Father is highly respected at the state university where he accepted a six-figure salary to be a professor. Mother is a neurologist and considered tops in her field. She took a six-figure job at a mid-sized hospital about twenty minutes away.

Then, there's me. Unlike my parents, I'm not respected or tops in my field. I'm simply a misfit, wandering around lost and friendless in this foreign world.

The cultural shift from my native country of Turkey to the United States is gigantic. Everything is so different. The food. The clothes. The music. The social structure. Everything.

Father and Mother return from their jobs every night and I can tell they're happy. They're always marveling at the opportunities in this country. I wish I felt the same way, but I don't.

They ask how things are going for me. I think about lying--telling them what they want to hear--but, instead, I tell the truth. I tell them how difficult it is, how I don't fit it, how I don't understand; that I don't have any friends.

They try to sympathize, but they don't get it. They keep talking about the "opportunities" we have here that we didn't have in Turkey. They tell me that soon I will adjust--that all of this is only temporary--that someday I will see what they're talking about.

So, I go to my room. I try listening to the radio as I finish my homework. I know the kids in my high school like the popular music playing, but I struggle to understand it.

I go to bed early. What else am I going to do? Call and socialize with friends I don't have?

So, I struggle to get out of my bed each morning. I search for some nugget of positivity that I might hold onto. Most days I don't find it.

I dress in the clothes that I brought with me from Turkey. A print button-down shirt with long sleeves, corduroy or canvas pants, black or grey socks, and a pair of brown loafers. My clothes are different from the T-shirts, jeans, and sneakers my classmates wear but I don't want to change them. These clothes are the only familiar things in my unfamiliar world.

My parents are usually gone in the morning, so I eat some cold cereal with milk then get dressed, comb my thick black hair, brush my teeth, put on my orange backpack, and head for school.

It's a lonely walk. I see other kids in groups--probably with friends they've known all their lives. Sometimes they brush past me on the sidewalk. They don't acknowledge me--just bustle along.

The inside of the brick school building is a lot like you'd imagine-- rowdy and chaotic. Kids socializing and traipsing all over the place. Everybody generally seems carefree and excitable. Of course, I'm the smallest kid in the place--not surprising-- since I'm way younger than everybody else. I don't feel any of this carefree excitement. I clutch the straps of my backpack and quietly go to my locker. Putting my backpack inside, I get the books for first hour. I sit alone in the classroom--the morning bell doesn't ring for another fifteen minutes. I try to look busy; like I don't notice I'm alone. I blankly stare at a page in some random textbook.

Sometimes Ms. Carroll, the teacher, comes in early.

"Good morning, Josef," she says with a smile. "How are you today?"

"Fine," I mutter.

"That's good. How are your classes going?"

"Fine."

"Getting used to your new surroundings?"

"Yes," I lie.

She sits down behind her big desk. She's probably the first and last person I'll talk to during the day.

I sit alone at lunch eating my ham sandwich, cheese stick, and applesauce. Thankfully nobody bullies or harasses me. I count down the minutes until lunch ends.

I can't wait for the day to conclude. Others hang around after school talking with friends. There is this boy/girl dynamic. It's not a whole lot different than how things were in Turkey. Of course, I'm too young for all that. Who has a girlfriend at age 12? Who'd like me anyway?

I go home directly. The house is quiet. My parents won't be home for another couple of hours. I could watch TV but I don't understand the lure of game shows. I could listen to the radio but I'm not used to the songs. I could do my homework, but then what would I do after supper to pass the time?

Sometimes I play with my Matchbox cars on the kitchen floor. Sometimes I practice on my Ukulele. Sometimes I get out my binoculars and watch the birds in the backyard. These things give me some enjoyment, but then I invariably think about school and wonder what my classmates would think about a high school sophomore playing with toys or gazing at a Scarlet Tanager.

There are 176 days in each school year. I've got three years left; that's 528 days of high school. A week from now it'll be down to 523.

See, being smart is really a curse; it'll probably ruin my life. I'm beginning to hate the idea of learning things because it's brought me nothing but difficulty. If my father was a street bum and my mother a simple housekeeper, I'd still be living in Turkey. I'd be with my friends. I wouldn't have "opportunities" but who cares? I don't want any more "opportunities".

Won't be long before everybody starts pushing me towards college. What do you want to go to college for, Josef? Neurology like your mom? Astrophysics? Genetic engineering? Yuck! I hate it all, but how do I tell my parents that?

 I can see myself going to some college a thousand miles away from this place. I'll end up sitting alone in some kind of apartment, shades drawn, flunking my classes, and surrounded by empty liquor bottles.

And you thought you had little to look forward to.

The reason to get out of bed today? It's Friday. It isn't much of an incentive but it's something to hang my hopes on. Only eight hours of school left 'til the weekend and two days without misery.

I eat breakfast alone and I walk to school alone. I walk down the hallway alone and sit in first hour alone. I eat lunch alone. A normal day for me.

Then comes last hour and I'm sitting in the back of the room...alone...

Mr. Jensen, history teacher, comes in and brings the class to order.

"Today is the day," he eagerly announces. "Today is the History Bowl."

History Bowl--Mr. Jensen has been talking about this for the last two weeks. It's where the sophomore history class competes against the senior history class for school bragging rights or something like that. Each class selects 5 members to represent their grade. The two groups of 5 then compete in a series of questions about US history--the team with the most correct questions is crowned "History Bowl Champions".

Apparently, according to Mr. Jensen, the History Bowl has been a lopsided affair lately; the seniors have won for the last six years. Should that be a surprise?

"First thing we need to do is select the sophomore representatives," Jensen announces.

"Tracy Higgins, please come up here," he says.

While Tracy climbs out of her seat, Jensen continues.

"At the risk of embarrassing Tracy, the reason I chose her to be team captain is that she has a perfect grade point average, and I'm guessing the sophomore class wants to have their best and brightest up against the seniors."

He gets no objections.

Tracy is in front of the class. This girl is my parallel opposite. She's a good looking American girl who everybody likes. She has friends wherever she goes. She is never alone. She'll be excited to go to college--probably will become an astrophysicist.

But enough thinking about her, because I've got another problem. The vaunted History Bowl will be held in the school auditorium. The representatives will sit behind tables on the stage with the remainder of the sophomore and senior classes sitting out in the crowd. What this means is it'll be like lunch with yours truly sitting all alone in some back row for the duration of the excruciating process.

"Now, Tracy, I need you to choose four other students to help represent the sophomore class," Jensen says, rubbing his hands together.

Tracy doesn't hesitate, "I want Josef."

This hits me like a loaded baseball bat. Did I hear correctly? Did she really say my name? I look up and see Mr. Jensen waving to me.

"C'mon up front, Josef."

The rest of the class kind of turns around and stares at me. Embarrassed, I climb out of my desk and timidly walk to the front of the class. I stand awkwardly next to Tracy. She catches my gaze and smiles. The first time since I arrived here, somebody other than a teacher has smiled at me.

My mind is racing as I stand there. Why would Tracy choose me over her gaggle of friends? Of course, we all know the answer. It's because I'm smart and we need smart people to beat the seniors.

The selection process continues. Charles Weston from the chess club is next, followed by Molly Tran, go-getter Korean exchange student, and finally Rachel Donald, mathematics whiz.

As a class, we head down to the auditorium. The senior class is already there. Their five reps are sitting behind a white table up on stage. The rest of the senior class is sitting in the first few rows.

Led by Tracy we head up on stage. We take our seats and I stare across at our opponents; a three boy two girl contingent of very scholarly looking seniors.

Standing between the tables of the two teams is a black metal podium where the moderator will conduct business.

There is a general buzz in the auditorium. Looking out at the back doors, I watch as rows and rows of rambunctious kids file in.

"Who are they?" I hear Molly ask Tracy.

"The seventh and eighth graders from the junior high," Tracy replies.

Well at least I'm not the only twelve-year-old in the building, I think to myself.

With the students and teachers finally settled, Mr. Jensen brings the place to order. I notice Mrs. Grandby, the school principal, is in attendance.

"Well, hello, and welcome to the fifteenth annual History Bowl," Jensen says.

I look out at the crowd. Everybody seems transfixed on the stage. Even the junior high kids are paying attention. I shift in my seat. How did I get in this spot? Another curse of being smart.

"....the moderator will ask a question," Jensen was saying. "Each team will then have a minute to confer among themselves and record the answer on the index cards provided on the table. When time is up, the captain of each team will offer an answer to the question. Each correct answer scores a point for the team. As time goes on, the questions will get progressively harder. At the end of twenty questions, the team with the most correct answers becomes the History Bowl champions....any questions?"

There was silence.

"OK, let's get started, first question: What year did the Mayflower land at Plymouth Rock?"

It was a relatively easy question and required little discussion. Tracy looked down the table.

"1620?" she asked.

Everybody nodded in agreement and she wrote the answer on an index card.

Both teams scored an easy point.

After ten questions we'd kept pace with the senior team and the score was tied.

"Alright teams, question 11: Who was President James Buchanan's Vice-President?"

There was a noticeable pause at my table. It was the first time uncertainty crept in. I watched as my teammate's eyes darted back and forth. Tracy kind of shrugged her shoulders and gave us a pleading look. Charles was mumbling to himself. Rachel hotly whispers that she doesn't know. Molly looks confused. That just leaves me, and of course, I know the answer.

"John C. Breckinridge," I state.

The other four stay quiet.

"Are you sure?" Tracy asked.

"100%," I say.

"Time's up," Jensen said, looking down at his stopwatch. "Seniors, what is your answer?"

The captain of the seniors, a hefty guy with thick glasses looked down at his index card.

"John Breckinridge," he announced confidently.

There is a nearly undetectable whoosh of relief that spreads across our table.

Jensen turns to us, "And sophomores?"

"John C. Breckinridge," Tracy replied.

Mr. Jensen paused for a second, purposely adding some drama.

"Both teams are correct."

Tracy looked at me and winked, "Good job, Josef."

Molly smiled and actually patted me on the leg.

It was an amazing feeling. I actually felt like I belonged; like I was part of a team. My confidence soared and I cracked a rare smile.

The competition continued. The questions kept coming and a strange thing began to happen. My four teammates seemed as if they were getting overwhelmed. After each question, they began turning to me for the answer which, of course, I provided.

The Magna Carta.

Howard Hughes.

1844.

Nelson Dewey.

The Abscam Scandal.

Pittsburgh Landing.

Humble Oil Company.

The Santa Fe Ring.

All answers provided by me. All of them are correct.

And, now, the stage was set. Last question, question 20, both teams tied at 19.

I briefly looked out at the crowd. The place was absolutely quiet, everybody's eyes still glued to the stage.

Jensen was obviously enjoying the high drama.

"OK, folks, we're tied at 19 a piece," he crowed. "And, now our final question, which may determine who will be crowned this year's History Bowl Champion: Who was the last person to step foot on the moon?"

The room went dead. Both teams began to quietly whisper.

Tracy Higgins looked down the length of the table.

"Well?"

Charles Weston, chess club extraordinaire, spoke first.

"I know this one," he said as his eyes lit up. "My family was just at Kennedy Space Center last summer. It's Gene Cernan, Commander of Apollo 17."

Rachel Donald nodded in agreement. Molly Tran shrugged her shoulders.

"Gene Cernan, then?" Tracy asked.

Gene Cernan was certainly a good guess, but it was wrong.

I chimed in.

"No, it's Harrison Schmitt."

This caused a noticeable hiccup at the table. Tracy was suddenly baffled.

"Well, which one do we use?" she asked urgently. "We gotta decide quickly."

"It's Ceran," Charles repeated sternly. "I know this one, swear-to-God."

Tracy looked at me with pleading eyes.

"Harrison Schmitt," I said.

This did not help matters at all.

"OK, time's up," Mr. Jensen announced.

We all watched as Tracy hastily scrawled something on the index card.

Jensen turned to the seniors, "Your answer?"

"Eugene Cernan," the senior Captain replied.

The tension ratcheted up at our table.

Jensen turned to Tracy.

"And sophomores?"

There was a small pause. I watched as Tracy stared down at the index card in front of her. She looked up.

"Uh, Harrison Schmitt?" She weakly answered.

Jensen was quiet, he remained expressionless and held things for a moment. The whole place seemed to be suspended in time.

"And the answer is... Eugene Cernan, Commander of Apollo 17," Jensen said.

The wind seemed to suck out of our side of the stage. Charles Weston growled under his breath.

"Congratulations, seniors," Mr. Jensen said. "By a score of 20 to 19 you are the History Bowl champions."

The senior table erupted, smiles, and high fives everywhere.

The crowd began to applaud, and Mr. Jensen walked over to congratulate the seniors.

But the thing was that he had the wrong answer. Actually, there were only two people in the auditorium who *had* the right answer. One was me for coming up with the correct name, and two was Tracy Higgins for writing it down.

I felt a surge of anger begin to boil inside me. If my life had been royally mucked up because I was so damn smart, I might as well prove my worth.

I slid my chair back from the table and stood up, my heart pounding.

"You're wrong," I said.

Nobody heard me.

"Excuse me," I announced louder. "YOU-ARE-WRONG!"

This caught the attention of Mr. Jensen and the celebrating seniors.

Jensen looked at me like I was bonkers. Guess this was out of the norm for the quiet, unnoticed twelve-year-old.

"Huh? What?" he asked.

"You've got the wrong answer," I stated. " The answer you have to the last question is wrong."

This kind of ebbed the mood on stage.

Mr. Jensen thought for a moment before he motioned for silence. In a very disjointed manner, the auditorium crowd and seniors retook their seats.

Complete silence reigned. Mr. Jensen retreated to his podium, looked at his papers for a moment, and then turned to me.

"Sorry, Josef, I don't know what to say. The answer is Eugene "Gene" Cernan, Apollo 17 Commander. He was the last person to stand on the surface of the moon."

I took a deep breath. I didn't want to be arrogant, but sometimes being smarter than everybody in the room can be very laborious.

"I know, but, could you please re-read the last question, sir?" I asked.

Mr. Jensen seemed a bit miffed as he looked down at the papers on the podium.

"The last question, question twenty was: who was the last person to step foot on the moon?"

Jensen looked at me, "And that was Gene Cernan, end-of-story."

"Well, not exactly," I replied. "Eugene Cernan was the last of the twelve moonwalkers to *stand* on the moon, but it was his fellow astronaut, Harrison Schmitt, who was the last person to *step foot* on the moon."

Mr. Jensen looked at me exasperated, "Huh? No, I don't think you understand, Josef."

I took a moment to look around. All eyes were focused on me. I proceeded in a measured response:

"OK, when the Lunar Module from Apollo 17 landed on the moon, NASA flight rules dictated that the Mission Commander, who was Eugene Cernan, be the first man to exit the module. Up until that time only 10 other men had stepped on the moon. When Cernan climbed down the ladder, he became the 11th man to *step foot* on the moon. Shortly thereafter, astronaut Harrison Schmitt exited the lunar module behind Cernan. When he stepped off the lunar module, he became the 12th and *last man to step foot* on the moon. So, the correct answer is Harrison Schmitt."

Nobody moved. Nobody said anything.

Mr. Jensen's eyes narrowed. I could see his mind spinning. His brow furrowed and he looked down at his papers. He mouthed the twentieth question to himself and then thought for a second. Slowly his expression changed, and the puzzled look left his face. He looked at me, smiled, and nodded.

"Very good, Josef, very good. You are absolutely right."

A murmur rippled through the auditorium. My teammates seemed stunned. I looked over at the senior table. They appeared utterly confused, but then the captain of the senior team caught Mr. Jensen's eyes. He nodded.

"The kid is right," he said.

Mr. Jensen retreated behind the podium. He took a deep breath.

"Folks, after some thought and reconsideration, there has been a change in the final results. The sophomore's answer to the last question was, indeed, correct. So, it's my pleasure to announce that this year's History Bowl Championship goes to the sophomore class. Congratulations."

Feeling a flood of relief, I took my seat at the table. Charles Weston patted me on the shoulder, "Good catch, Josef."

"That was awesome," Molly Tran said, squeezing my leg again.

"Remind me to never doubt you," Rachel Donald said smiling.

Tracy Higgins got up, walked over, and gave me a hug.

"Great job, Josef."

That afternoon I walked down the sidewalk towards home, clutching the straps to my backpack. It had been a good day. As I thought about it, a small smile began to form.

Behind me, I heard the quick patter of rubber soles on the sidewalk--somebody obviously in a hurry. I stepped over to let them pass, but as they grew closer they slowed down. I looked over. It was Charles Weston. He smiled and stopped.

"Hey Josef, how'd you know that answer?"

I thought for a moment, "I don't know. I guess I'm just smart."

"Well, it was pretty cool...say, you know anything about chess? The team could use a smart person like you."

I looked up. The warm sun hit my face. I shielded my eyes. I smiled.

"Yeah, I think I'd like that."

JOHN LORY

The Three Forces

T'was in the waning days of the year and, as had become the custom, three very important beings commenced their annual meeting. The purpose of this once-a-year sojourn was to indulge in food and spirits well into the night and discuss their dominion over the earth.

So it was that the three, referring to themselves as The Three Forces, agreed to join around a laden table in a fancy meeting hall at the appointed time.

The first of the Three Forces to arrive and settle was the buxom lady known as Mother Nature. Enthralled with all the beauty the natural world could offer, Mother Nature adorned herself in the finest deep orange silk dress with cuffs and collar of subtle evergreen. She powdered her round ruddy cheeks, parted her golden hair in the middle, and fashioned a tiara of bright fragrant flowers and sprigs of spearmint, which she placed on her head.

The second member of the resplendent trio to appear at the meeting was a cold foreboding figure known as the Grim Reaper. The Grim did not desire the fine accouterments worn by Mother Nature but instead chose simplicity. He expertly concealed his hideous countenance under a thick, tattered, dull, black hooded cape. Grim's duties required that he walk a great deal, and barely visible beneath the hem of the Grim's cape were dusty, black, cracked leather boots with tarnished buckles and worn soles that scraped ominously with each step he took. Latched firmly in his bony left hand, he carried the trusted instrument of his trade: a large scythe with a worn and knotted oak handle and a broad, sharp, gleaming blade.

The last one of the Forces to arrive was the oldest member of the guild, a dignified man known as Father Time. Still a regal and confident being, despite his advanced years, Father Time dressed in a shimmering white gown with twinkling silver sequins. His etched and bronzed face sported a long wispy beard of pure white, tapered and manicured to absolute perfection. For this occasion, he wore upon his head a snow-white top hat with a white silk ribbon, and in his right hand, he carried a sleek crystal staff that was six inches taller than his own upright, noble frame.

The Three Forces, a proud and imposing trio, greeted each other lavishly and took their seats around the table. As they consumed rich food and expensive drink, they beguiled one another with all the pertinent news of the past year. Mother Nature and Grim focused much of their dialogue on the misery and hardship they perpetrated upon the hapless men and women who inhabited the earth, while Father Time, as was his nature, remained far more reserved and quiet.

As the night progressed and the drink flowed, the self-effacing, pleasant atmosphere began to fade, and soon a cloud of deep melancholy settled over the room. It was then, that the conversation took a sharp turn, and the Forces found themselves lamenting past failures.

Heavy into her spirits and suffering a rare case of doldrums, Mother Nature began relating a pensive tale from many years ago which, until this evening, she'd kept deeply hidden in the recesses of her mind.

She told the tale of a group of men, a baker's dozen to be exact, who late one evening ventured out onto a calm sea aboard a small wooden vessel. Mother Nature, who was in a malicious mood that particular night, stated that she looked down on this group of seafarers and elected to bedevil them. She called up a hurricane wind and a hard drenching rain which she sent against the boat. She then unleashed a torrent of mighty white-capped waves, intending to splinter the wooden vessel and send it, and the men who occupied it, into the watery depths. It was with added indignance, then, when she noticed that although *twelve* of the men struggled with her fury, the thirteenth one quietly slept at the bow of the boat. Mother Nature sought to punish the apparent nonchalance of the thirteenth man, so she commanded the wind to blow with more vigor, the rain to pelt harder, and the waves to grow in size and ferocity. She then confidently watched as the twelve men began to labor harder, struggling to maintain their course, and fighting to salvage their very lives. Through it all, though, despite the tossing of the vessel and the raging of the elements, the thirteenth man still remained asleep. In short order, however, despite the best efforts of the courageous twelve, the boat was dashed to and fro in the froth and began to swamp and tilt. With all hope nearly lost, it was then that the accursed men began to cry out, appealing for assistance from the one who calmly rested at the bow. Their desperate voices somehow pierced the roar of the maelstrom, and the thirteenth man awoke. It was then, Mother Nature confided, that she witnessed what she'd originally thought impossible. The thirteenth man rose up from his resting spot with an impressive aura, and although the boat was being lashed and tormented by violence, the strife failed to hinder this man. Fear did not become him and hopelessness did not envelope him. Standing stoically at the front of the boat, with his companions watching, he called out to the very wind, water, and waves that sought to destroy the boat. His voice and rebuke were strong and he resolutely commanded the winds to stop their fury, the rain to cease and retreat, and the waves to settle at once. Much to Mother Nature's surprise and utter amazement, the change was immediate. The elements whimpered and bowed to this man's wishes, disappearing from the water as quickly as they'd arrived. Then, without as much as a twist of a breeze remaining, the mysterious man and his companions proceeded on their trek across the sea wholly unimpeded.

Having finished her story, Mother Nature soberly queried her companions for a reasonable answer as to how a sleepy fisherman of no renown could best both her and the terrible array of natural forces at her disposal.

Silence overtook the table. It was then that Grim, who seemed unsettled by the tale, steadied himself on his chair, and broke the hush when he tepidly declared that he, too, had an incident in his past, not dissimilar from Mother Nature's, where his seemingly unchecked prowess had been blunted.

Grim began his oratory:

He reminisced of a time, far in the past, while in the process of carrying out his customary daily duties, a rather nondescript man of simple means captured his attention. Grim, who possessed among his wide array of powers the ability to read the hearts and minds of mortals, revealed to his counterparts that this man, without reservation, carried both a heart and mind of unequaled virtue, patience, compassion, wisdom, and love. Grim also stated that he'd detected a deeper tenor to the man, but it was something he could not place.

As fate would have it, years later, this humble man was condemned on a charge bearing no merit and suffered an unjust and abominable death. Remembering the intrigue that had drawn his interest in this man previously, Grim went forth to collect the man's soul for the afterlife but, curiously, could not find it.

Puzzled, the Grim Reaper meticulously scoured the far reaches of the netherworld searching for the man's soul but, alas, the quest ended in frustrating failure. It was three days later, then, to the shock of Grim, when this man defied all natural order, broke the ironclad grip of death, and returned from the depths of the grave to reclaim his place back with the living as if he were a conquering king.

Tale told, Grim turned towards Father Time and Mother Nature and invited interpretation. How had a simple and humble man, apparently limited in means, thwarted the absolute of death, unhanded the clutches of the grave, and came back to life?

Again, silence enveloped the Three Forces.

Father Time had his own notions about the stories that had been recently shared. He conceived things in a different light, for he had traits that neither Mother Nature nor The Grim Reaper possessed. Time had afforded him the gift of experience, the luxury of wisdom, and the keen ability to meditate and ponder.

Father Time was cognizant of Mother Nature's beginnings and those of The Grim Reaper, for he'd been present when they'd been introduced into the world. However, as he spent time reflecting, he realized that he had virtually no knowledge of his own origin. His original hypothesis had been that he *just was*; a lone ethereal being. For centuries upon centuries, Father Time, with hourglass and staff in hand, strode unhindered across a silky, dark, formless earth in the belief that he was alone and that all the earth was his sole domain. That very impression was challenged one day, in startling fashion, when strange events began to unfold. It started with the appearance of a shining light that broke through the black murk. Then, in rapid succession, the sky, oceans, and dry land appeared. These drastic changes were troublesome for Father Time as, for the first time in his existence, events were transpiring that he could not explain.

While Father Time grappled with the change, plants and vegetation appeared, followed by a host of creatures on the ground, in the air, and in the water. Things concluded with the arrival of two human beings in a garden.

The once formless planet had been transformed into a paradise of indescribable beauty--a true masterpiece. Father Time's trepidation slowly eased when he finally realized that he was not the ultimate power in the world nor the one who controlled the earth. At night, as he stared up at a panorama of twinkling stars, a pause of wonderment filled him. A magnificent creator was out there, unencumbered by time and space, and who held all in his powerful hands.

For a brief moment, Father Time considered telling his thoughts to Mother Nature and Grim, for he was convinced that the one who created the earth was also the same one who had rebuked Mother Nature's maelstrom and defied Grim's domain of death.

But, were his comrades ready to hear this revelation? Were they ready to put down their pride and concede that, despite their broad powers, they were still subject to an all-powerful being?

 He looked hard at Mother Nature and Grim, contemplating. Finally, with a measure of reluctance, he decided to hold his tongue. It wasn't time and he knew that the other two, regardless of the evidence, would certainly reject the idea of an almighty Creator.

The two of them had much to learn. Maybe they'd be ready at next year's meeting....

Johnny Lee Dillard

What kind of person has snapshots of young kids tacked up on their wall? What kind of person has a cache of weapons and a Confederate flag hanging hidden inside a walk-in closet? I don't know, but Johnny Lee Dillard has all of those things.

Johnny Lee Dillard is my next-door neighbor. I know his name because one night an NRA flyer blew out of his recycling and landed in my yard. Ever get that feeling when you just know something is amiss--something is wrong? Yeah, that's me concerning Johnny Lee Dillard. The name pretty much confirmed things--my next-door neighbor is some kind of white supremacist pervert.

Now, I'm not a busybody or shit-stirrer or anything like that. I generally don't care who my neighbors are or what they do. I'm content to mind my own business, but Johnny Lee Dillard is different.

Late one night, I was up in my attic looking at a waxing gibbous moon through my telescope when the light flickered on in the back room of Johnny Lee Dillard's house.

At first, I thought nothing of it, but when a drifting late night cloud wandered in front of the moon blocking my view, I gazed down at the light. Because of my unique elevation, I was able to get a pretty distinct view of Johnny Lee Dillard's life.

Ol' Johnny Lee's back was to me; stringy gray hair and a dirty white tank top. He was hunched over some sort of desk or table undoubtedly doing some nefarious activity. However, what captured my attention was what was above him on the wall. There were seven or eight snapshots of young kids haphazardly tacked to the off-white drywall by multi-colored stickpins. That seemed kind of odd to me.

Forgetting the moon, I began to concentrate a bit more closely. That's when I noticed the closet to Johnny Lee's right. The brown bi-fold doors were thrown open and best I could tell there was a Confederate flag--stars and bars--hanging on the back wall. This unnerved me a bit, so I swung the telescope away from the heavens and focused it on Dillard's backroom. After a bit of twisting and focusing, I managed to get a magnified view of my neighbor's room. What I saw horrified me.

As Johnny Lee continued his labor-intensive work at the table, I got a close-up view of things. There were eight photos on the wall--five little girls; three little boys. All were Latino. I ticked the telescope a bit to the right, focusing on the closet. Thanks to the enhanced magnification not only did I get a close-up of the Confederate flag, but I was privy to Dillard's arsenal of previously unnoticed weaponry. A cache of rifles, handguns, and long knives were neatly mounted on the wall next to the damnable rebel flag. The sight sent shivers down my spine. Who was this ghoul?

Then, Johnny Lee was up. His sudden movement caused my heart to jump. For a moment, I thought I'd been discovered but quickly realized I was too far away for Dillard to notice. I settled and watched scruffy Johnny Lee shuffle away from whatever he was doing previously and partially disappear into the closet. He bent over in the corner for a moment. I couldn't see what he was doing, but shortly thereafter, he backed out of the closet lugging a tattered brown suitcase with leather straps and tarnished brass buckles. He plunked the thing down in the middle of the floor. Intrigued, I quickly adjusted the telescope. Dillard opened the ancient case. I couldn't see what was in it until he shifted slightly. The thing was full of odd-looking instruments--some bright and shiny; some dull and old. Dillard pulled out a long wicked looking saw and gently caressed the handle. I was shocked. I'd seen a saw like it once before. It was when I was a kid growing up on the farm. What Dillard was holding was a bone saw. My grandfather had used the one on the farm to cut up a hog on butchering day. What Johnny Lee Dillard planned to do with his was still a mystery.

Like the crazed lunatic he was, Dillard, gently one-by-one, removed various instruments of torture from the suitcase. He inspected each one before placing it on the wooden floor. He treated the instruments with the utmost care as if they were alive as if they were his pets as if he were somehow in love with them. It was as sick as it was and fascinating, and for about a half-hour I watched Johnny Lee Dillard and his macabre routine. Only after he stood up and closed the curtains did my reconnaissance end.

That night, I couldn't sleep. I rolled and wallowed and shifted in my bed thinking the whole time about my psycho neighbor. What on earth was going on? What should I do about it?

 Early the next morning, hot coffee in hand, I climbed back up into the attic. I slid open my telescope window and stared down at Johnny Lee Dillard's quiet home. The curtain to his room of evil was still closed. However, something else caught my eye--in Dillard's backyard. There were four random holes that had been recently dug into the green grass--piles of fresh dirt sitting next to each wide hole. This both did and did not surprise me. Holes in the backyard? It kind of fit in with the whole scenario I'd watched unfold the previous night. It was pretty apparent that Johnny Lee Dillard was up to no good.

As I finished my coffee and retreated back down the stairs, I realized that I was in an unenviable position. By pure happenstance, I'd stumbled onto something and now had a decision to make. One, I could just ignore things. What Johnny Lee was doing was none of my business. In fact, if I hadn't been up in my attic the previous night, I wouldn't have a clue about the late-night activities of one Johnny Lee Dillard. Two, I could tell somebody about what I uncovered. I thought about guys like Gacy and Bundy. How many people could've been saved if somebody had said something instead of ignoring the signs? What if the police had been alerted earlier in those cases?

I struggled with what to do most of the day. Ultimately, after work, I decided to be a good citizen and stop at the police station.

The on-duty sergeant at the front desk seemed unfazed when I gave him a brief synopsis of what my neighbor was up to. He instructed me to take a seat on a beat-up vinyl chair in a dirty lobby with thumbprint smudged windows and promised to get somebody I could talk to "as soon as possible".

As soon as possible turned into a good 75-minute wait. At long last, a tired-looking chap with a mismatched brown suit and loose crooked tie appeared from the back of the precinct. He was chubby and balding with a thick mustache and yellowed teeth. He announced that he was Detective Marks, blandly shook my hand, and led me back to a cramped office with a desk stacked with manila file folders.

As Marks rearranged the mess on his desk, he offered me a seat in a dilapidated, plaid wingback chair that looked as tired as he did. I eased into the chair and watched as Marks took a seat behind his desk. Peering at me between stacks of folders, he sighed and asked what he could do to help me.

Finally, the moment I had been waiting for! In rapid fashion, I reeled off my fantastic tale. Worried about the possible implications of spying on somebody with a telescope, I led Detective Marks to believe that I'd witnessed all of Johnny Lee Dillard's actions with my bare eyes.

Marks remained stoic and patient as I relayed my story, infrequently making eye contact and writing nothing down.

When I finished, I expected some decisive action by the detective, but he did nothing.

"So, did you witness this Dillard fellow actually harming another person?" Marks asked.

"Well, no, just the pictures of the kids on the wall."

"Has Dillard threatened you or anybody you're aware of either with or without these weapons you claim he has in his possession?"

"Uh, well, no...not that I'm aware of anyway."

There was a moment of silence. The detective looked down at his desk, then back up at me. He sighed again.

"Well, Mister...uh..."

"Carver, Jeff Carver," I quickly inserted.

"Well, mister Carver, thanks for stopping in," Marks said. "I'll file a report on this so we have a record of your concerns."

I was stunned at his lackadaisical response.

"Aren't you going to do something? Aren't you going to come out and see for yourself; at least knock on Dillard's door and talk to him? Something?"

"Well, to be honest, Mr. Carver, your neighbor...this Dillard guy... hasn't broken any laws, and based on your description hasn't done anything wrong. We just can't go knocking on doors and demanding things without proper proof."

"...but the pictures...the flag...the weapons...you can't do anything?"

"Not based on what you've told me. Now, if you had some concrete proof or come across something more substantial then perhaps there is something we could do."

I was floored. There was nothing they could do? A criminal operating right under their noses and they chose to be passive?

Disappointed, I left the police station with nothing but Detective Marks' business card.

When I pulled into my driveway, I stopped outside of the garage and stared at Dillard's big white two-story house. I felt a flicker of anger. Why was evil allowed to have free reign?

I angrily tossed Marks' business card onto my bare counter. I tried to console myself as I ate supper and watched TV. Hey, I did my duty. I saw something and reported it; let the authorities know. The fact that they chose to do *exactly nothing* was not my problem. Perhaps, someday, when several missing children were unearthed in Dillard's backyard then the police, Detective Marks in particular, would see the folly of their attitude.

Someday, on the local news, there'd be a shaky camera recording of Johnny Lee Dillard, head down, being led out of his front door in handcuffs. There'd be the startling revelation that a predator had been living in a quiet neighborhood. They'd interview people who'd describe Dillard as the clichéd "quiet loner who pretty much kept to himself".

Yes, Dillard had fooled them all--except for Jeff Carver. But, Carver's concerns fell on deaf ears. Detective Marks had been too busy to take Carver's reports seriously. Oh, the children who were needlessly murdered because of that slight!

It'd be a small measure of vindication. Too little too late.

It was another restless night. My mind mulled over the things I'd seen in Dillard's house and my conversation with the Detective. I kept hearing Marks' words over and over in my head, *"Now if you had some concrete proof or come across something more substantial then perhaps there is something we could do."*

Maybe there was something I could do. Maybe there was a way to get some "concrete proof".

For the next couple of weeks, I made my way up to the attic at dark and trained my telescope on Dillard's window. To my dismay, the curtain remained closed and the light off.

Each morning, I bounded back up to the attic and scouted the backyard. Again, to my dismay, the four holes remained inactive.

I began to discreetly track Johnny Lee's movements. It appeared as if he was a working man with regular hours. Monday thru Friday, at about 7 AM, he'd leave his house, driving a rusty red pickup. From behind the slats in my mini-blinds, I saw that he wore some kind of uniform with a name tag. It indicated to me that he was a blue-collar worker--perhaps a janitor or maintenance worker at an industrial company or hospital.

He returned home around 5 PM every night. He'd hit the button on the door to his one-car garage and disappear inside. I rarely saw him on nights and weekends. One Saturday he did leave at about 6 AM and didn't return 'til early evening, but other than that--nothing.

Then one night, as I lay in my bed, obsessing over Johnny Lee Killer and his life, I decided to make my move. Get the "concrete proof" Detective Marks desired.

I'd call in sick one morning and then wait for Dillard to leave for the day. I'd then break into his house and discover what he was up to.

Now, I knew breaking and entering was a serious crime, but that infraction would be overlooked once the world was alerted to the crimes of Johnny Lee Dillard.

Like a stir-crazy cat, I waited that particular Friday morning. I'd gotten up early, phoned my boss, reported a migraine headache and stomach problems, and began my recon of Dillard's house.

After three cups of coffee, nervously checking the clock every two minutes, and peeking through the blinds, I was finally rewarded when Dillard's garage door chugged open and the uniform-clad Johnny Lee hopped into his truck.

I eagerly watched as he maneuvered out of the garage, shut the door, backed out into the street, and disappeared from view.

Confident that the predator would be absent until late in the afternoon, I sprung into action.

I left my house, marched over to Dillard's, and walked up to the front door. I pressed the doorbell several times and pounded on the entrance. This was all part of my carefully planned ruse.

I was certain that Dillard lived alone. However, to cover all bases, I'd devised this ploy. If I was surprised and somebody magically appeared at the door, I'd simply introduce myself as the next-door-neighbor, explain that the power was out in my house, and inquire if they were experiencing any like problems. When they informed me all was well in their house, I'd simply retreat back home and make alternate plans for another day.

Fortunately, and as planned, nobody appeared at Dillard's front door. Satisfied that the place was empty, I quickly returned home. Next, I slithered out of my back door and looked around. My neighborhood was remarkably quiet. I bent down and quickly jogged over to the back of Dillard's house. I was in such a hurry rounding the corner, I nearly ran smack dab into four unplanted saplings sitting next to the house, their tender roots covered with wet gunny sacks full of dirt. Skirting the trees, I tried the storm door at the back of the house. To my pleasant surprise, it opened. I descended ten rickety steps to the basement door. I grabbed the handle and pushed it. For a second, I thought I'd hit the jackpot as the door started to open. However, after about three inches, it stopped. Using my smartphone flashlight and twisting my neck at an unnatural angle, I was able to see that the door was being held secure by a small hook and latch.

Swearing under my breath, I quickly made my way out of Dillard's basement stairwell, and back to my own garage, where I grabbed a metal coat hanger. Like a gazelle, I returned to Dillard's back door without incident.

In the muddy light, I straightened the hanger, bent it at what I felt was an appropriate angle, and stuck it in the door crack in an attempt to lift the hook out of the latch. This operation took several attempts but I was finally rewarded when the hanger caught. With a quick jerk, I lifted the hook out of the latch.

I slid into Dillard's musty rock foundation basement and flipped on my flashlight. A quick sweep with my light revealed the typical basement--furnace, water heater, a few non-descript plastic totes, and a couple of storage shelves. Across the room was an open stairway ascending to the main level.

I walked to that stairwell and climbed the creaky steps. At the top, I gently pushed open a thick wooden door, and just like that, I was standing in Johnny Lee Dillard's kitchen.

Bright sunlight filtered through Dillard's dusty windows and I extinguished my phone's flashlight and stuffed it in my pocket.

Dillard's decor was stuck firmly in the late '70s. Harvest gold countertops, dark brown cabinets, gaudy white and brown peel 'n stick tiles on the floors. Aged wallpaper sagged on the walls; a refrigerator hummed quietly. There was a strong smell of Lysol cleaner; the counters and sink were empty.

I skirted past a small table, ducked under one of those stupid '70's chandeliers hanging by a cheap brass chain, and plugged into a wall outlet. I wandered down a shag carpet hallway, past a couple of bedrooms, a bathroom, and stopped at the end of the hallway.

In front of me was a battered brown door. If my calculations were correct, this was the room I'd viewed from my attic perch. I took a deep breath before turning the handle. What horrors might I find behind the battered door? I steeled myself and gritted my teeth.

With a quick burst, I pushed the door. It swung open and banged lazily against the wall. Feeling brave, I flipped on the light switch.

There were no surprises or grisly revelations. The room was neat and uncluttered.

Anxious to discover something, I made my way over to the table and chair that Dillard had been using the night I'd watched him through my telescope. Sitting on the table was a map with little push pins sticking in it. My first thought was that Dillard was possibly marking out spots of his former crimes or the locations of his buried victims. I was about to take out my phone and document my find when I gave the map a closer look. It was a detailed map of the state of Virginia. Next to the little push pins were neatly written names like "Sharpsburg" and "Manassas"-- Civil War battle sites. Hardly the kind of evidence I was searching for.

Undaunted, I looked up at the children's pictures tacked to the walls--all eight of them. On closer inspection, I saw that the Compassion International logo was at the bottom of all eight pictures. A few of the photos had handwritten notes on them. *"Thanks for your support, Mr. Dillard." "Your generosity makes such a difference!" God bless you always."* I blanched a bit. Apparently, Johnny Lee Dillard was sending monthly financial support to eight disadvantaged kids in third world countries around the globe.

Slowly, my adrenaline began to ebb. The investigation was progressing in a far different direction than I'd expected.

Hoping yet to nail Dillard, I flung open the closet. There hanging on the back wall, in all its glory, was a Confederate flag, and just like I'd seen through the telescope, an assortment of weaponry was hanging on the wall. Strangely, the weapons looked like antiques. The rifles were something called *muzzleloading Springfields*. The handguns were equally old things called *Navy Colts*; the long knife I'd spied from a distance was some kind of sword with a fancy but functional hilt. It was tucked into a long slender scabbard. While I was contemplating the meaning of this, I was puzzled to find another flag in the closet. This was a United States flag, neatly folded in a triangle and sitting on a shelf. Below the folded flag, on the hanger rack, were two neatly pressed suits--complete with hats. The first was navy blue; the second butternut gray. They were both military uniforms.

What was the meaning of this?

I looked back on the shelf. Sitting next to the folded flag, facedown, was a wooden picture frame. I grabbed it. The black and white photo featured several men--all in Civil War dress. In the middle was Johnny Lee Dillard, his long gray hair unmistakable under his hat.

Again, at the bottom of the picture was a handwritten note. *"Cheers Capt. Dillard. Whether Union or Confederate you're still a great commander."*

Then it hit me. Johnny Lee Dillard was a Civil War reenactor!

I'd read about these reenactors before. They were basically Civil War nuts who, along with other similar nuts, attended historical events and partook in mock Civil War "battles". They dressed up either as Union soldiers or Confederate soldiers as needed. A strange hobby to be sure, but far from anything insidious.

Suddenly, I felt like a first-class fool. I cringed as I thought about all the time I'd obsessed over this man; how I'd been in a hurry for the cops to bust down his door and toss him in jail. What a moron I'd been.

Looking down in the corner of the closet, I spied Dillard's mysterious case full of instruments. I didn't open it for I now knew what was inside--Civil War field surgeon tools.

I swallowed hard and felt guilt wash over me. I carefully and soberly put everything back the way I found it, and giving the smiling faces of the third world kids Johnny Lee Dillard was giving hope to, I closed the door to the room.

I retreated to the basement and latched the back door. Returning upstairs, I quietly slipped out a side door, locking it behind me.

At home, I was at a loss of what to do. I wished I could make things up to Johnny Lee Dillard; apologize for being a horse's ass. But, how could I do that? Leave a phone message?

Sorry, Mr. Dillard. I was spying on you and mistakenly deduced you were a white supremacist, serial killer pedophile. Sorry, I narked on you to the police. Hope you can forgive me.

I thought of the absurdity of that for a moment before I got an idea. I grabbed my laptop and opened it. I looked up Compassion International and stared at the smiling kid on the homepage. Thirty-eight bucks a month to give a poor kid real hope.

Perhaps if Johnny Lee Dillard could quietly make a difference in this world then so could I.

JOHN LORY

The Catch Of A Lifetime

Eddie Staley quickly looked around at his teammates in the huddle and then turned his attention to the quarterback. It was late autumn and a spectacularly warm and humid day. His team, the Mount Ralston Stallions, were engaged in battle with the Columbus Bearcats for the Junior College Division VI Championship.

The game had been a rough seesaw affair with multiple lead changes, but presently the Stallions found themselves trailing by five points with only eight seconds left on the clock. The ball was spotted on the 32-yard line--32 yards of green turf between the Stallions and a championship.

Three plays earlier, the Stallions' All-Conference quarterback had been knocked out of the game with a semi-serious concussion and the keys to the team and its fortunes had been thrown into the lap of a very green freshman.

Eddie looked at the young quarterback's clean white uniform which stood in stark contrast to the soiled and scuffed jerseys of the rest of the team. He looked into the wide, unsure eyes and watched the nervous drumming of the young man's fingers on his thigh pads. This was not good.

The rookie quarterback began to stutter as he tried to call out the play. That's when Eddie took over. A four-year starter at wide receiver, Eddie had been in many big games and he knew stage fright when he saw it. He reached over and firmly grasped the right wrist of his quarterback.

"Get it together, man," he said, glaring at the youngster. "This'll be the last play of the game, which means it's also the last play of my college career, so we're going to do things right. Forget about the play coach sent in; this is what you're going to do. Hike the ball on two, take a five-step-drop, and launch the ball towards the south corner of the end zone. That's where I'll be, and I promise you by everything good in this world I *will* catch that ball."

The new quarterback half-nodded and let out a deep breath.

"You got it? You all got it?" Eddie addressed the team.

The rest of the players clapped their hands together, broke the huddle, and walked up to the line. Eddie split out wide and took his stance. He looked back at the ball, watching it twitch ever so slowly in the hand of the center. He glanced up at the skinny, rawboned kid playing quarterback. Then the center hiked the ball.

Eddie took off. A quick hitch caused the defensive back to lurch, and just like that, Eddie was past him and racing towards the corner of the end zone.

When he looked back, he saw a wobbling football, high in the sky, coming in his general direction. His eyes narrowed, focusing on the ball. He could feel the sweltering swirling heat around him and the sting of the sweat leaking into his eyes. And then the whole world went dead. All sound disappeared, and his surroundings melted away. It was just him and that fluttering football. His shoes found purchase in the turf and his legs began to surge. He moved towards the ball in a singular fluid motion; his entire body responding to the task at hand. At the last second, he left his feet and extended his arms fully, snatching the ball out of the air mere seconds before it hit the ground. His body crashed to the turf with a thud, but his well-trained hands kept a steady, vice-like grip on the ball.

Then, like magic, the world returned. The crowd was roaring, his teammates were crowding around him, helmets off, cheering, yowling, and thumping each other on the shoulder pads. A big lumbering lineman reached down, grabbed Eddie by the front of the jersey, and easily yanked him to his feet. The big guy embraced him in a giant, crushing bearhug.

"Eddie, you the man," he growled into the earhole in Eddie's helmet.

Escaping his teammate's hug and still holding the ball in one hand, Eddie pulled off his helmet and joined in the celebration. The moment was more than he could have imagined. He'd done it. He'd led his team to victory on the biggest stage of his career.

Seeing the greenhorn quarterback in the bubbling crowd of exuberant humanity, Eddie pushed through them and with a twinkle in his eye, flipped the ball to the youngster.

That'd been twenty-five years ago.

Since then, things had gone steadily downhill for Eddie Staley. Freshly out of college, he first tried his hand at football. Not nearly good enough for the NFL, Eddie got a couple of tryouts with an Arena Football team, and a cup of coffee in an independent league, but he soon realized that he was just a small, forgettable fish in a very big pond. Seemed like there was always somebody who was stronger, taller, faster, or smarter than him. Eddie could catch a football pretty good; others could catch it better.

He left the sports world and tried putting his communications degree to good use. He failed. There was only a spattering of jobs, and once again Eddie was faced with the reality that the world was full of other people with communication degrees who employers seemed to prefer over him.

His love life didn't fare much better. He bounced around with a few different girlfriends. A couple of times Eddie thought he might have something special, but inevitably the relationships dissolved and his world fell into mundane.

When he was younger, he'd envisioned himself playing for the Green Bay Packers; he ended up working as a general laborer for Green Lawn Landscaping. His seemingly aimless life weighed hard on him and he wondered where he made the wrong turn.

At night, unable to sleep, he'd sit in his recliner and stare off into space, thinking. Thinking about what used to be back when he was in junior college. Thinking about all those late afternoons spent on the practice field catching footballs out of the JUGS machine. Hours and hours of practice. Catch one, catch another, then another. Again and again and again. Camping under the balls shot high up into the air. Waiting, watching, judging the subtle wind patterns. Catch one, catch another, then another.

He looked down at his hands; the hands of a thousand footballs. But now, they were rough, cracked, embedded with dirt, and destined to sling sod 'til the end of time.

'Til the end of time.

It was spectacularly hot that August afternoon. The unrelenting sun was making things miserable and the rake Eddie was using to clean up the client's yard felt wet and greasy in his hands. It had been a particularly long day of mowing, raking, and collecting yard waste. A red utility truck with the dump bed full to the brim with grass clippings sat at the curb, evidence of the day's long hard work. Eddie's job partner for the day, a fat slop named Baker, was slumped under a maple tree soaked with sweat.

"C'mon Staley," Baker said, twisting open a bottle of Mountain Dew. "It's break time. Get outta that sun before you roast."

Eddie nodded. "Yeah, just a second. I want to finish up this little bit of lawn."

He turned back to his work and that's when he heard the police siren. It was faint at first but began to grow louder. Eddie stopped his raking and watched as Baker wallowed to his feet and hiked up his low hanging pants. Both of them watched as a police cruiser sped by and slid around the corner at the next intersection.

"Must be something going on," Baker said. "I'm gonna go have a look."

Eddie didn't reply. It was a police car. So what? Seemed Baker would do almost anything to get out of work.

A few moments later, an ambulance screamed down the road and turned at the same intersection as the police car. This perked Eddie's interest. He put down the rake and walked out to the street.

The first thing he saw was Baker lumbering down the sidewalk as fast as his fat toad-like legs would carry him. He anxiously waved, so Eddie started down the sidewalk wondering what had him so bothered.

When he reached Baker, the fat man was unable to speak. Apparently, exertion got the best of him. He bent over and sucked in a couple of large big gulps of the humid air.

"What's going on?" Eddie asked.

Baker finally stood upright. His face was crimson red and sweat was dripping off of his saggy jowls. He chugged a few more breaths and placed his hands on his jumbo-sized waist.

"Fire," he gulped. "Fire next block over; three-story apartment building up in flames."

This alarmed Eddie, and without a word, he quickly started down the sidewalk. Baker groaned and fell in behind him.

When Eddie rounded the corner, he saw the fire. Just like Baker had reported; a three-story apartment complex, clad in beige siding and white trim, was ablaze--the orange flames spiking up into the air.

Two police cars and an ambulance with flashing lights were on the chaotic scene and a growing crowd of people were milling around.

"Where the hell is the fire department!" a distressed lady with crazy gray hair was addressing a young police officer. "There are people still in that building for God's sake!"

"Ma'am, the fire department is on their way. Now, please do us a favor and move out of the way."

"But there's still a woman trapped in there!" the lady roared. "She's gonna burn to death if somebody doesn't do something now!"

The cop brushed past her and hurried towards the burning structure.

By now, Baker had caught up. He and Eddie surveyed the scene. Thick smoke was rolling out of the doors and windows of the building as the dancing flames blackened and bubbled the vinyl siding. There were people stumbling out of the complex doors, coughing, and wheezing as they fought for clear air. A couple of EMT's were directing the escaping patrons away from the burning building. But what captured Eddie's attention was what was going on at the edge of the building. A corner window on the third floor was open and amid the billowing smoke, Eddie saw a frantic lady leaning out and screaming. Below, at ground level on the broken asphalt parking lot, were two cops. One of them had a blue and white bullhorn in his hand and he was trying to communicate with the lady.

This made Eddie uneasy. Concerned, he quickly made his way over to the corner of the building. The cops didn't notice his arrival. That's when Eddie saw that the lady was holding something in her arms.

"Ma'am, you gotta calm down," the cop with the bullhorn was bawling. "The fire department will be here soon. Just hang on...we'll get you and your baby out."

The lady was having none of it.

"Please, help us!" she screamed. "Please help my baby!

Eddie looked up at the desperate woman and the package she held in her arms. It was then that something clicked inside him and suddenly he knew what to do. He quickly turned to Baker, grabbing him by the wrist.

"I need you to run your butt back to that house as fast as you can, and bring the work truck on the double, OK?"

"Huh?" Baker said, confused. "What do we need the truck for?"

"I don't have time to explain," Eddie barked. "Just do it, OK? As fast as you can. It's a matter of life and death for that lady up there."

Baker seemed to catch the seriousness of the situation and using a gear Eddie didn't know he had, Baker bustled away.

Eddie then went back over to the cops under the window.

This time, one of them stepped into his path.

"Sir, get away from here, now!"

"Just a minute," Eddie said. "I know what to do. I can help. I know how to save them."

The cop just shook his head and began to push Eddie away. That's when the officer with the bullhorn stopped trying to calm the lady in the window and turned to Eddie.

"What's that you said, son?"

"I know how to save them," Eddie said. "But we gotta move fast. Here give me that bullhorn."

Seemingly confused, the cop gave the bullhorn to Eddie and stepped back.

Looking at the wailing lady hanging precariously on the window sill bathed in gray smoke, Eddie hit the button.

"Ma'am, ma'am, I need you to listen to me, OK?"

The lady ignored him and continued her frantic rambling.

"Dammit, lady!" Eddie shouted. "If you would just SHUT UP for a minute, I can tell you how to save yourself and your baby, but you gotta listen."

His abrasive tone caused the lady to stop bawling and for a moment there was silence except for the cracking of the fire.

"Now listen and listen good," Eddie said. "I can save you, but we gotta move fast, OK?"

The wide-eyed lady gave a weak nod.

"Now what you need to do is wrap that blanket around your baby as tight as possible. Then you're going to have to toss him down here and I'll catch him."

The lady seemed repulsed by Eddie's idea. She clutched her baby tight to her chest and shook her head back and forth.

"No way, I'm not going to do that. I can't. I just can't drop my baby."

"Listen lady, it's the only way," Eddie called back. "It'll be OK. I promise you by everything good in this world I *will* catch your baby."

The lady hesitated for a moment.

"C'mon lady," one of the cops encouraged. "It's a good plan. You'll be OK."

A small crowd of people had now gathered. Some of them began to call up to the lady, offering encouragement.

After a brief moment, the trapped woman seemed to respond. She carefully unwrapped part of the blanket, pulled it tight around her baby, and tucked it in. She then gave the child a quick peck on the forehead and forlornly looked down. Then with a sigh and gasp, she tossed the package.

Eddie watched the little baby, tightly wrapped in a brown blanket, come floating towards him. His eyes narrowed, focusing. He could feel the sweltering swirling heat around him and the sting of the sweat leaking into his eyes. And then the whole world went dead. All sound disappeared and his surroundings melted away. It was just him and that little helpless child. And in that fleeting moment he finally understood why he'd spent all those hours on the practice field; why he had worked so hard to perfect his craft; why God had given him the hands that caught a thousand footballs. Eddie's shoes found purchase on the hot asphalt and his legs began to surge. He moved towards the baby in a singular fluid motion; his entire body responding to the task at hand. At the last second he left his feet, and extending his arms fully, he snatched the child out of the air mere seconds before the package reached the ground. His full body crashed to the faded blacktop with a mighty thud, but his well-trained hands kept a steady, vice-like grip on the child.

Then, like magic, the world returned. People were clapping and cheering. Still on the ground, Eddie handed the baby to one of the police officers. He then shot to his feet, ignoring the red road rash on his forearms.

Where was Baker?

He spotted the work truck idling in the middle of the street. Dodging through the cheering spectators, he quickly made his way out to the truck. He jerked open the door and ordered a mildly surprised Baker to slide over.

Eddie jumped behind the wheel, put the truck into gear, hopped the curb, and skidded to a stop in the parking lot. One of the cops had since figured out what he was going to do and was busy herding people out of the way.

Eddie threw the truck into reverse and with the assistance of the helpful cop, he quickly backed up underneath the window of the stranded lady. In a jiffy, he hopped out and motioned to get the lady's attention.

"Alright, Miss, your turn," Eddie said.

She was scared out of her wits and looked like she'd just been asked to jump into a bottomless pit.

"Miss, you'll be OK," Eddie reassured her. "There are about four feet of grass clippings in the truck; it's no different than jumping on a really big mattress. Now c'mon your baby is down here waiting. You both can be reunited in less than a second."

A big poof of black smoke swelled out of the open window. It was enough to convince the lady to move. She crawled out onto the ledge and with a shrill screech, she jumped. It wasn't graceful, but she landed harmlessly in the mound of grass clippings. She floundered around for a bit before one of the police officers helped her out of the back. She was handed her baby.

About this time, a large red fire engine roared up to the apartment building. Eddie and Baker, now lost in the chaos, got back into the truck and returned to their yard work.

Two weeks later, Eddie was trimming weeds at a curb when a boxy teal car pulled up and stopped. A woman climbed out. Eddie looked up. It took him a moment to realize it was the lady from the apartment fire. She looked quite different when not frantic and plastered with black soot and grass clippings.

She smiled and walked over.

"Hey, you remember me?" she asked.

Eddie nodded.

"Well, I just wanted to thank you for what you did for me and my baby," she said.

Eddie shrugged, "It wasn't much."

"Yeah, right," she smiled again. "By the way my name is Lisa."

A year-and-a-half later, Eddie and Lisa were married--and sometimes late at night, they talk about the crazy way they met and found love.

Lisa says Eddie is charmed. She tells him that most guys can only dream about catching a last-second touchdown to win a championship or dramatically saving a damsel in distress from a burning building, but he's the lucky lout who actually got to do both.

Eddie just smiles when she says that and usually doesn't have much to say. But, occasionally, he thinks about the catches in his life--he's got a definite top three: 3-A wobbly touchdown pass; 2-A little baby tightly wrapped in a blanket; 1-Lisa--his greatest catch ever.

The Electric Man

Boyd felt a nervous twitch inside himself when he pulled into the parking lot of Neptune's Gentleman's Club. This would be a new experience for him and he didn't know what to expect.

He observed the parking lot. The pea gravel had been washed away by summer rainstorms and a winter's worth of snow plowing; it was a mess of ruts and potholes. The club building was sad, and generally mirrored the condition of the parking lot. The storm gray paint covering the outside of the clapboard siding was weathered and chalky from age. A rotted, lopsided split rail fence--missing some critical pieces--languished out front. Untended flower beds--full of dead weeds--flanked both sides of a dark tinted glass front door. A half-dead, neon Bud Light sign blinked in one of the windows, and a couple of rolling dumpsters, both overflowing with garbage, were sloppily placed at one corner of the building.

The whole place screamed dilapidated desperation, except for the sign over the entrance--a big teal and white backlit monstrosity, announcing that one was now entering Neptune's Gentleman's Club.

Boyd decided to park in the back of the establishment for obvious reasons. Although he didn't exactly live in a small town, there was always the off chance that somebody who knew his truck might drive by and that could eventually lead to a lot of rumors and uncomfortable questions.

When he exited the truck, he instantly felt the soggy despair that surrounded the place. It was almost enough to make him get back into the truck and leave, but he'd already come this far, might as well keep going.

He pulled the obstinate front door open and slipped inside. He was greeted with a muddy boots/stale beer smell, and he took a moment to let his eyes adjust to the dark interior. To his right was the performance stage--an elevated area with dirty white peel 'n stick tiles on the floor and a tarnished brass pole bolted to the ceiling. The evening's entertainment had not yet begun and the wooden chairs in front of the stage were mostly empty.

To his left was the bar; a long wooden counter with a brass foot rail and cheap Naugahyde covered bar stools randomly placed in front of it.

Nobody paid him any mind, and he was at a loss about what to do. Where did one go in this place? What did they do?

He decided his best move was to head up to the bar. He took a seat on one of the stools and rested his forearms on the sticky counter. Now what? There was no bartender; there were no waitresses, just the sick rattle of an overtaxed air conditioning unit and some kind of pseudo dance/rap music sputtering out of a pair of flyspeck covered speakers on little shelves behind the bar.

When his phone unexpectedly dinged, he nearly jumped out of his skin. He dug it out of his pocket. It was a text from his wife.

Where are you? She asked.

Working late, be home sometime. He typed.

We're having Jake's B-day party tonight--don't forget. She wrote.

Be home ASAP. Busy day. He replied.

He waited a few moments. He received no further correspondence, so he stuffed the phone back into his pocket.

When he looked up, he saw a woman appear from the smoky darkness of the small bistro table area. She sauntered toward him. At first, he thought perhaps she was the bartender or a waitress. She was neither.

She was an aged and weathered blonde, desperately trying to cling to her yesteryears. She was packed into tight jeans a couple sizes too small, a low cut, cleavage-revealing white top, and black, calf-high, mock leather boots.

His heart began to pound as she came closer. Was this really happening?

Without a shred of reluctance, she slid onto a barstool next to him. She smelled of cigarettes and cheap perfume. Tired eyes, saggy cheeks, wrinkles hidden under a layer of makeup. She offered a sultry oft-practiced smile. Her teeth were wide gapped and discolored.

He didn't know what to do and his mind began to tumble random thoughts. Why was a lady frequenting a gentlemen's club? Why did she set up shop right next to him? What did she want?

Of course, he knew the answers to these questions. This was to be expected when one visited a place called Neptune's Gentlemen's Club.

Nervous, he nodded at her.

"First time here, honey," she purred.

He cleared his suddenly stuffy throat, "Um, yes, it is."

"Well, I've got some advice for you," she leaned close to him. "You might want to remove that wedding ring if you're going to be in here."

Her words stung and embarrassed he looked down at the gold band on his left hand. Yeah, good as time as any, he thought. Quickly and roughly, he pulled the ring off and dropped it in the front pocket of his button-down shirt.

"Now, you're all set--a true free agent," she said, with a heavy smoker's laugh. "You wanna buy a lady a drink?"

He didn't know what to say or do--this was brand new territory for him.

"There's no bartender," was the only thing he could think to say.

The blonde cackled lightly. "Hey, Marty, get out here."

A couple of seconds later a sloppy man with a pockmarked face, graying hair, and thick glasses wandered out of a little room behind the bar. He had a stained white towel slung over his left shoulder; his blue T-shirt was threadbare and dirty.

"Whaddya want, Judes," he bellowed at the lady.

"You've got a new customer," she crowed. "Think he wants to buy a girl a drink."

Marty removed the towel from his shoulder.

"Well, what'll it be, fellow?" he asked.

"Um, actually, I'm here on business," Boyd said. "Southside Electric. We got a call from you guys earlier?"

"Oh, yeah," Marty said, slapping the towel back on his shoulder. "Wondered if you guys were gonna show. Backroom lights and damn freezer ain't working. You wanna talk to Clyde. Here, follow me."

As Boyd got up, he gave a short glance to Judes. Her mouth was half open and she looked offended.

He followed Marty into a dingy back hallway that reeked of urine and tobacco. Marty led Boyd into a dark-paneled room with a DIY desk, a ratty swivel chair, yellow shag carpet, and a water-stained drop ceiling.

"Clyde'll be here soon," Marty said. "Have a seat if you want."

Boyd looked briefly at the cracked leather loveseat in front of the desk. He elected to remain standing.

Marty plodded off to find Clyde, leaving Boyd alone in the office.

Boyd was regretting the choice to come here.

If only he hadn't been so considerate.

Less than an hour ago, he was heading out the door at work, his day over, when the boss called out to him.

"Boyd, can you do me a real solid?"

He had really wanted to go home, but Dale, his boss, had always been a stand-up guy.

"What's up, Dale?"

"Just got a call from Neptune's," Dale said. "They got some kind of problem in their backroom--something about a freezer and backroom lights, I think...Look, I know it's Friday afternoon and all, but could you swing by there and check it out?"

"Can't wait, huh?"

"Apparently not," Dale said, scratching his chin. "Weekend is their busy time. They need the freezer and lights up."

"And they couldn't have called earlier in the day?"

"It's a strip club," Dale shrugged. "Look, I know it sucks, but I'll make it up to you next Friday--give you the afternoon off with pay, huh?"

"Yeah, OK," Boyd said reluctantly. "I'll stop by and see what I can do."

"Thanks a bunch," Dale smiled. "Have a good weekend, OK."

"Yeah, you too," Boyd replied with a quick wave.

Now, here he was standing in the backroom of Neptune's waiting. Hopefully, Clark, or Clive, or what's-his-face would show up soon. Jake's birthday was tonight.

A few minutes later a fat, sweaty man, in a black sequin button-down and gray polyester bell-bottoms bowled into the office.

"You the electric man then?" he inquired.

Boyd tried to not stare at his terrible Vegas-esque lounge outfit, "That I am," he smiled.

"Clyde Drubbly," the guy said, holding out a meaty paw.

Boyd gingerly shook his grimy hand.

"Follow me," Clyde said, marching out of the office. "Problem with the backroom; no lights, an' the freezer don't work."

Boyd fell in and Clyde led him down another musty colorless hallway lit only by a few naked 40-watt bulbs. They stopped outside a dark room. Reaching into the room, Clyde vigorously flipped the light switch up and down a half-dozen times.

"See, the lights ain't working and neither is the freezer."

Boyd pulled a flashlight off of his belt, flicked it on, and quickly scanned the dark room.

"And the breaker box? You know where that's at?" Boyd inquired.

"Sure do," Clyde said, confidently. "Right this way."

He led Boyd around a corner and pointed at a couple of gray boxes on a dirty and bare wall.

"Smaller one of them two boxes," he said. "That's the one Phipps was messin' around with the other day."

Boyd skirted past Clyde and popped open the smaller box.

"I'll take a look and see what I can do," he said.

119

"Dancin' starts in about an hour," Clyde said, looking down at a gold watch on his fat wrist. "Be great if things are workin' by then."

"All right, I'll see what I can figure out. By the way, you got a rear exit in this place? My work truck is parked out back."

Clyde pointed to a rusty steel door. "That'll take you out back. Don't worry none, it doesn't lock."

"Thanks," Boyd said.

"Well OK, then," Clyde replied after an awkward moment. "I'll let you get to it."

Sequin shirt twinkling in the substandard light, Clyde headed back towards his office.

Thankful to finally be alone, Boyd went out to his truck using the beaten up back door. At the truck, Boyd opened the center console and pulled out a navy blue ring box. He then fished his wedding ring out of his front pocket, carefully placed it in the box, and put the box back into the center console.

A few years earlier, he'd been on a job with an amiable fellow named Riggins. In a rare, careless moment, Riggins accidentally touched a live wire. As the shot of electricity knocked him off his feet, Riggins instantly grabbed his hand and started screaming in pain. Turns out, the electricity had arced to his wedding ring; the heat had practically melted the thing into his finger, and Riggins had to have it surgically removed. Ever since he'd witnessed that, Boyd never wore his wedding ring while in the field.

Back inside Neptune's, he removed the front panel of the box and bathed the innards with his flashlight. The thing was an unholy snarled mess of wires--likely none of it up to NEC standards.

Fortunately, Boyd found the problem quickly. Apparently, Phipps (whoever that was) must've knocked a hot wire loose while he was "messin' around" in the box.

Boyd smiled to himself. At least it was an easy fix. Shutting off the main, he located the proper breaker, reattached the wire, and put the panel back together. He flipped the breakers and then retreated to the offending room. He hit the light switch and a bank of fluorescent lights stuttered and hummed as they came alive. The compressor on the dirty, old, stainless steel freezer began to buzz and whine. Problem solved.

Boyd took his tools to the truck, put his wedding ring back on, and returned to the back of the club. Now, where was Clyde?

As he wandered up the smellway to Clyde's office, he thought about telling him that the freezer should be on its own dedicated circuit and that the panel was in dire need of reorganization. The mouse that scurried across the hall in front of him changed his mind. No sense in telling the captain of the Titanic about a cracked window pane in the second class dining room.

Clyde was in his office, seated at his desk, barking angrily at somebody on the phone. When Boyd popped his head in, Clyde lowered the phone and covered the mouthpiece.

"All set, just a loose wire," Boyd said. "We'll bill you."

Clyde nodded, and unceremoniously returned to his phone call.

Boyd turned, aiming to avoid the main room and exit out of the back door. Unfortunately, halfway down the back hall, two scantily clad women were having a loud argument. After trading unrepeatable insults the two began slapping each other and pulling hair.

No way was Boyd going to get in the middle of that.

Frustrated, he turned and started off the other way, eventually coming out next to the bar in the main room.

Judes was still parked at the counter. Her devious eyes lit up at the sight of him.

"So, you ready to buy me that drink, Mr. Electric Man?" she croaked.

He looked at the sorry old hag for a moment.

"No," he curtly replied. "I'm not buying you anything."

She began to stutter out some retort, but Boyd wasn't listening. He pushed his way out of the joint, feeling like he was leaving a sewer.

His workweek was over.

Thankfully, he'd be home in time for Jake's party.

The Fink

The one old lady told the other old lady that she needed to get a bottle of Spring Valley western dressing because Annie was coming for the weekend and she liked that particular kind of dressing.

Brent Wilder didn't really know what western dressing was nor did he care. He also didn't like the fact that he was bottlenecked behind the two old chattering bats as they entered the narrow sliding doors of the grocery store.

He impatiently shuffled behind them and as soon as humanly possible, he weaseled past the ladies and hurried into the store.

Beer was what Brent needed and he didn't have time to plod behind some bitty blabbering about Annie's weekend visit and her western dressing fetish. Stupid people!

He skirted past a couple of people pushing carts and around a giant flabby man sagging over the sides of a motorized shopping cart.

As he shot down one of the long aisles contemplating what brand of beer to buy, something caught his eye and he came to an abrupt stop.

There in front of him, sitting on a chest-high shelf, was an actual bottle of Spring Valley western dressing. How ironic, he mused. Brent grabbed the glass bottle and inspected it. So this was western dressing, huh? This was what Annie the weekend visitor liked? Some gross, thick, goopy, slop? What the hell did you do with it anyway?

Brent shook his head and placed the bottle back on the shelf. As he did, he noticed that the Spring Valley western dressing was a *"Hot Buy"* this week, and providing that the lucky customer had the right coupon and was also a *Quik Rewards* member, the dressing could be purchased for a buck cheaper than normal.

Apparently, this deal was quite appealing because the Spring Valley western dressing had been snapped up by the general public at an alarming clip, and only a single bottle remained.

Brent was thinking about this odd fact when the two old ladies who'd blocked his way into the store slothed around the corner pushing a nearly empty shopping cart. Brent gave the ladies a closer look. They were similar in appearance and stature-- probably siblings. Both were shriveled and bony with white hair and liver-spotted skin. One of them had horn-rimmed glasses and both of them wore heavy windbreakers--clearly unnecessary on the warm April afternoon. It was a pathetic sight.

He watched the two crawl down the aisle, and that was when he got an idea. With a wicked grin, he snatched up the last bottle of Spring Valley western dressing and quickly moved into the next aisle where he stuffed it behind a row of boxed macaroni and cheese.

Annie would not be enjoying her favorite dressing this weekend.

Satisfied with this slight, Brent made his way to the liquor department and picked up a twelve-pack of Bud Light. Heading up to the checkouts, Brent couldn't resist retracing his steps back through the dressing aisle.

He was pleased to see that the two old women were still there. They had parked their cart in front of the salad dressings and were looking up and down in a vain effort to locate a bottle of Spring Valley western dressing.

An evil smile tugged at Brent's lips as he shifted the twelve-pack into his other hand and prepared to skirt past the ladies' cart.

He was almost around them when one of the ladies looked up and her eyes locked with his.

"Excuse me, sir," she said. "Could I get you to help us out for a second?"

Brent growled inside. It'd been a stupid and arrogant move to come back through the dressing aisle. He should've just gone another way.

Nevertheless, he was now in a mess of sorts that he'd created. Feigning concern, he looked at the ladies and shrugged.

"We're looking for a bottle of Spring Valley western dressing," the lady said, "but we can't seem to find it."

"Uh, well...okay," Brent replied, shifting the beer again.

"My niece, Annie, is coming for the weekend," she continued. "Spring Valley western is her favorite."

"Yeah, um... I'm guessing they're probably out of it," Brent said, thinking about the bottle hidden behind the macaroni and cheese in the next row. "Probably that empty spot on the shelf."

He gave an ambiguous nod with his chin in the direction of the empty shelf space.

The other lady, the one who hadn't spoken yet, tottered over and squinted as she read the shelf label.

"Right here, Midge," she said, disappointed. "See? They're out of it."

Midge huffed.

There was an awkward moment of silence.

"Well, looks like you're right, young man. They're out of stock," Midge finally said. "But, thanks for your help, anyway."

"Yep," Brent replied.

He began to walk away but was suddenly hit with an devilish dose of inspiration. He stopped, turned around, and shifted the beer again.

"Hey, I think they might have some of that stuff up by the checkouts," he said. "I thought I saw it up there earlier. You might want to go up and see."

"Oh, you think?" Midge asked, seeming to perk.

"Yeah, I'm pretty sure," Brent replied.

"OK, thank you, son," Midge replied, warmly. She then turned to her companion. "He says there is some more up at the front."

Brent smirked inside, hurried down the aisle, and around the corner.

As he finished checking out, Brent looked over his shoulder. Here came Midge and her sister slowly shuffling up towards the checkouts, searching for a stupid bottle of dressing that wasn't going to be there.

Inside his car, Brent popped open a can of Bud Light. He took a long drink and felt utter satisfaction spread over him. He thought about the two old women in their ridiculous windbreakers meandering through the store like a couple of lost waifs searching for a silly bottle of dressing that, incidentally, they would never find. That'd teach 'um for slowing him down; for getting in his way and cramping his day.

Brent turned the key and brought his three-year-old Camaro to life. He revved the engine and reveled in its throaty rumble. Driving in the loud red and white beast gave him an air of superiority. His car was faster, shinier, and louder than what the average ham and egger drove. He'd installed a loud thumping sound system and spent extra to have vanity plates that read BW ROX.

Finishing up the beer, he tossed the can into the backseat and popped another. He turned up the stereo and jerked out of the parking lot.

Brent Wilder sped down the four-lane street, one hand on the wheel and the other holding a fresh beer. Coming upon a string of slow-moving cars, Brent swerved into the left lane and hammered on the accelerator. The Camaro roared past them all in short order. With a smug smile, he looked as the line of cars grew smaller in the rearview mirror. He was the king of the road.

Brent enjoyed the next couple minutes of weaving in and out of the slower traffic, losing count of the number of cars he passed.

His music was so loud, that he almost didn't hear the dinging noise. When he realized his phone was chirping, he put his beer into the cupholder, unbuckled the seatbelt, and fished the phone out of his front pocket.

He reattached his seatbelt and looked down at the screen. He'd received a text. Splitting his time between the road in front of him and the phone, he brought up the text. It was from his buddy, Larry.

Yo bro what up? Larry's text read.

Smokin' bitches in the Camaro fool... got great story 2 tell 2 nite, Brent quickly texted back.

When he looked up, he saw an orange sign alongside the road informing motorists that a ½ mile ahead the left lane was ending and all vehicles should merge to the right. Seeing that traffic was already backing up in the right lane, Brent sped into the left lane and floored the Camaro; he'd get ahead of all the slowpokes.

Again, there was another orange sign, this one read: LEFT lane ends, merge RIGHT. Brent looked over at the long line of slow cars to his right. He looked up ahead. The left lane was still open despite the warning signs. No sense getting over just yet.

The phone dinged again--another message from Larry. He glanced down to quickly read it.

When he brought his eyes back up to the road, he was horrified to see a large white truck with a big rusty Mansfield bar sitting dead still in the lane directly in front of him.

Brent stood on his brakes. He felt the pulse in the pedal as the ABS kicked in. Rigid arms and pounding heart, Brent watched the back end of the truck grow closer at an alarming rate.

It took Brent Wilder a moment to comprehend what had just happened. Slowly, he came out of his fog. With the limited mobility available to his left hand, he fought the deployed airbag out of his face. He then tried to move his right hand but it was pinned between the seat and center console; thankfully it did not hurt. Through the droopy remains of the airbag, he could see that the crooked bent steering wheel was a mere six inches from his chest--that was lucky. The taut seatbelt cut into his shoulder and prevented him from making any meaningful movements. Brent shook the cobwebs out of his head. Slowly, the fragmented pieces of the last couple of minutes began to take shape in his mind.

Flying down the road...a text from Larry....white truck....brakes...boom.

Brent began to angrily wiggle in his seat, attempting to free himself from the restraints. As he did, he felt something wet and slimy splat on his forehead. Alarmed, he shifted his eyes upward. Another wet splat hit his forehead. Slowly, things came into focus. There was a big white plastic barrel resting awkwardly on the crumpled hood of the Camaro. It was tilted backward and one end was partially sticking through a large jagged hole in the spider-cracked windshield. The barrel was leaking something and it was dripping onto Brent's forehead.

Splat, another fat drop. Brent felt the thick ooze begin to trickle down his cheek. Splat. He tried to move his right hand to wipe off his forehead. No luck. He tried the same thing with his left hand, but the seatbelt prevented it from reaching far enough. Brent tried to shift his head, but his current predicament only allowed for a minuscule amount of movement. He twisted a bit. The dripping stuff was now hitting his right cheek. After a few moments of struggling, Brent returned to his original position, resigned that for the foreseeable future he was captive to the steady dripping coming from the barrel. Splat...splat...splat.

Although it was less than five minutes, he felt as if he had been trapped for hours. He angrily began to count each time the goo from the leaking barrel dripped onto his forehead. One..two...three...four...five.

"Son...son? Can you hear me? Are you OK?"

A man in a blue button-down shirt was leaning down and staring at Brent through the cracked driver's window.

"Yeah, I'm OK, I guess...well mostly," Brent croaked. "I'm kinda trapped in here--my right arm is stuck and I can't move much...there's some kind of...of crap dripping on my head."

"Hang tight," the man said. "We'll have you out of there shortly."

Brent sighed. Like he had any choice in the matter.

A couple of firefighters in full gear arrived on the scene. They started up a wicked-looking saw. The goop continued to drip down Brent's face as the loud saw chewed through the hinges of the Camaro's door.

Once the door had been removed, a mini fight ensued with the steering wheel. Meanwhile, the dripping liquid slowly trickled down Brent's cheek and onto his top lip. Curious, he slowly stuck out his tongue. The ooze was thick with sort of a zesty/salty flavor. It didn't taste bad.

A half-hour later, after some gentle maneuvering, the seatbelt had been cut and Brent's trapped hand had been freed. He was spirited out of the mangled car and plunked down in the back of an ambulance. In a mild daze, Brent said nothing as an amiable

EMT threw a blanket over his shoulders, gave him a quick checkup, and handed him a bleachy smelling white towel to clean off his face.

"Just sit tight for a second," the EMT told him. "We'll be taking you to the hospital shortly."

The EMT hopped out of the back of the ambulance leaving Brent temporarily alone. Brent vigorously scrubbed the towel across his face to remove the sticky liquid slop. When he was done, he stared at the white towel now soiled with streaks and spots of dark orange. He tossed it onto the floor and cinched the blanket back around his shoulders. As he did, he heard a couple of people talking just out of his eyesight around the corner of the ambulance. He focused to pick up their conversation.

"So what happened, then?"

"Well, Sarge, looks like the hotshot kid in the red Camaro was flying down the road speeding, drinking, and texting all at the same time. Ignored the signs to merge and ended up smacking headlong into the stopped food truck."

"Kid was drinking?"

"Yep, open beer cans in the car."

"And texting?"

"Looks like it."

"Stupid, huh? Lucky to be alive if you ask me."

"I'd say. Totally destroyed the car and get this...looks like the idiot's insurance had lapsed."

"What? How you know that?"

"Found the proof-of-insurance card on the floor. Had to pick it out of a pool of that western dressing that was leaking outta the barrel sticking through his windshield."

"Western dressing?"

"Yep, western dressing."

The Purple Navigator

I'm sure that her Facebook page presented the myth of a perfect life. She was the kind of person who wanted to show the less-than-perfect people of the world that she had it going on; that she was better than them, and that if they had any sense, they would wish upon the stars that they could have it as good as she did.

It was easy to see that this was the case just by casually watching her from afar.

Shortly before 3 PM, on normal school days, the makeshift, rutted gravel parking lot across from the high school began to fill with vehicles. There were no painted lines in this lot to designate individual parking spots, but the majority of the patrons managed to park in a sensible and orderly fashion. But, then, she would arrive, soaring into the parking lot, behind the wheel of her gaudy purple Lincoln Navigator.

She did not park in the same rows as the mere mortals did, for she was above all of that--her purple Lincoln obvious proof that she was indeed on a different plane than the rest of the world. She created her own personal, reserved parking spot right at the very mouth of the lone exit. Day after day, she would ease the

Navigator off to the left side of the exit, one half parked on the scrub grass; the other half hogging two-thirds of the exit road.

As she sat there, she always left her purple colossus running, ensuring that her pampered self remained warm on those chilly winter days and equally cool on those humid, sunny spring afternoons. She spent a great deal of time on her phone as she waited for her child, the chosen one, to emerge from the school. She would multi-task; chattering about her important life to some anonymous person while peering into the little lighted mirror on the inside of the sun visor, and idly picking at her teased bangs.

Apparently, she felt as if it were her exclusive birthright to be the first one to leave the parking lot each day. Should a lesser human want to exit, they could either choose to wait behind her until she was ready to leave, or carefully attempt to maneuver past the Lincoln without scraping the side of another legally parked vehicle. She cared not which option they ultimately chose for others simply didn't matter.

Then, a few minutes after 3 PM each afternoon, trumpets would sound from the heavens, bright lights would pierce the parting clouds and her child, a young man of impeccable and noble stock, would emerge from the quiet confines of the high school. The collective breath of the earth would pause and rose petals would rain from the sky as *the gift* sauntered towards his mommy and her glorious purple ride.

Only after he'd climbed in and the Navigator had pulled out of the parking lot could the structure of time and space return to normal, and the rest of the average people could carry on with the process of collecting their mundane un-original kids and driving them to their equally uninspiring homesteads.

So, for days upon days, the peasants of the parking lot surrendered their worlds to the Queen and her purple Lincoln Navigator.

Then, came that December day. The day when nature blew in like a freight train and the whiles of winter unleashed a mighty torrent of snow. By 3 in the afternoon great gobs of heavy snow had piled up in the old parking lot, wreaking havoc. Vehicles of all sizes and colors spun, slid, and fishtailed around as they struggled to lurch into their random parking spots.

Then, as was the norm, the purple Navigator arrived. And, as was the norm, the Queen wound through the snarl and took her customary spot at the exit. As droves of snow continued to fall, she gazed into her lighted sun visor mirror and delicately applied a thin layer of designer lipstick to her perfect lips. The dull thud of her music could be heard over the hum of the afternoon, and her windshield wipers methodically slapped back and forth on the Navigator's windshield.

Then, at the usual time, the chosen one exited the high school building. The thick snowflakes were an unwelcome nuisance to him, and with his head down, he hurried towards the salvation of the purple Lincoln, daintily tiptoeing best he could through the thick layer of snow. Reaching the Navigator, he quickly slid into the passenger seat. His mother hardly acknowledged his arrival and spent a moment more viewing her exquisite countenance in the little mirror. Satisfied that she was at least the equal of Helen of Troy, the Queen shifted the Navigator into drive and stepped on the accelerator. The big back tires, mounted on custom rims, greedily spun in the slop, but the vehicle did not move. Irritated at this slight, she pressed down harder on the accelerator. The tires continued to spin madly, but the Navigator refused to budge. This lack of movement befuddled her. Things always responded to her whims and desires. Pressing down the gas pedal meant instant forward movement. How dare the Lincoln defy her wishes!

Soon, the back-up tail lights illuminated and once again the tires began to spin, this time in the opposite direction. The vehicle slowly began to move but, unfortunately, it was not in the direction desired by its commander-in-chief. The front end began to hop and slide and in only a few seconds of time, it slid down into a frozen rut packed with snow and became hopelessly stuck.

After a few more futile attempts, both backward and forward, the spinning tires ceased, and the driver's side window slowly lowered. The Queen stuck her head out into the elements and looked to and fro as if this simple act would magically solve her current problem. The snow fluttering into her face soon became too much; her head disappeared into the vehicle and the window slid shut. She tried to move forward. She tried moving backward. She did not move an inch in any direction.

Her quandary soon began to impact the rest of the parking lot. As she'd skidded back and forth like a fool, several mortals had collected their children and were aiming to leave the lot. Unfortunately for them, the wide back end of the purple Lincoln Navigator was now completely blocking the exit. The line of waiting vehicles grew as the frantic Lincoln continued to grind away, back and forth, the front end sliding deeper into the snow.

Soon, an old silver Chevy pick-up with rusty wheels and a bent front bumper made a move. Locked in four-wheel-drive, the Chevy expertly skirted past the wallowing Lincoln. It's aggressive tires cut into the wide snowbank to the right of the original exit. Chewing through the bank, the old truck soon hopped the curb, rolled onto the busy street, and disappeared from view. Seeing the new opening that the truck had carved, a blue SUV followed suit. Soon the steady line of cars began to utilize the makeshift exit. One-by-one they all made their way out of the parking lot, ignoring the floundering purple Navigator, and going about the business of their own lives.

Sunset

It's now the fall of '59...no, not 1959; 2059.

Although a lot of things have changed over my time (no, we don't have flying cars yet) a lot of things have remained the same. Getting old still sucks--I know that from experience.

I'm a rickety old man now--nearly ninety-years-old and my best days are far behind me, despite what some people think. Like that young, well-meaning woman I ran into the other day. She said I was in "pretty good shape" for my age. Hell, I don't feel like I'm in good shape--my entire body perpetually hurts, and just about everything I have--everything I care about--is now gone.

Denise, my wife, died a couple of weeks back. I knew it was coming but that didn't make it any easier. See, we met when we were teenagers--she was eighteen; I was nineteen. We'd been together for over 70 years. She was my life. Now she's gone. And, what exactly do I have left to live for? The world has passed me by. The kids have moved away and I'm left alone in this old house.

Now my son and daughter--a couple of good kids--said I should think about sorting through my stuff. Get things organized. Think about selling the house and moving into some retirement condo or some such thing. I know they're right, but this house holds the last vestiges of my Denise. We built our lives in this place.

I know that time will eventually take the house away from me, but I'm not going down with a fight.

I'm just a stubborn old man, stuck inside this monotonous life, with nothing to look forward to. Things would have stayed that way too if it hadn't been for the dream.

That particular night, I tottered off to bed with my usual cases of loneliness and despair. Of course, I couldn't sleep. My back hurt. My hip hurt. My head hurt. My soul hurt. I wallowed around in the bed for a few unproductive hours before I made my way out to the living room and plopped down in my old recliner.

I sat there alone, in the darkness, kept company only by the ghostly ticking of the clock. My mind, naturally, turned to Denise and like any old fool with nothing left to live for, I began to think about the past. I wished I could go back and relive life. Savor the good times a bit more--find a way to avoid those costly pitfalls.

Eventually, I drifted off into an uneasy slumber and that's when the dream came...

I woke up on a brilliantly sunny morning in my childhood bedroom on the family farm.

The first thing I noticed was that I felt good. Not an ache or pain or soreness anywhere, and my mind was clear and unencumbered by worry. The next thing I noticed were my eyes. I could focus and see clearly--no thick eyeglasses perched on the bridge of my nose. I could see the Chicago Cubs calendar on the wall distinctly and crisply. My dream had taken me back nearly 76 years; it was September 1983 and I was thirteen again.

Feeling a bit of wonderment, I pulled back the thin patchwork blanket and saw I was wearing my orange Houston Astros pajama bottoms. There was something bulky and uncomfortable in the front pocket. I reached in and pulled out my cell phone!

Dreams. It's mystifying how they can seamlessly mish-mash together the random and incompatible things hidden away in one's mind. A cell phone in 1983? Impossible unless you're in the middle of a dream.

I spritely climbed out of bed and found everything exactly the way it'd been 76 years ago. I felt myself easily falling back into my old routine. My clothes were on the chair by the bed. I pulled them on and tied my sneakers. Everything around me, every detail, seemed normal and appropriate--except for the cell phone.

Denise had given me the phone for Christmas a few years earlier. It was one of those new Holophones that had just become the newest and hottest tech gadget. Initially, I wasn't that interested in the thing; I was happy with the old touchscreen model my son had gotten for me. But, Denise said that the Holophone would be much better. She synced my voice (somehow) to it and now with a few voice commands, I could bring the thing to life--it's screen projecting out in front of me in a 3-D hologram. To placate her, I begrudgingly learned how to use it. And, although I'd never admitted it to her, I found the phone kind of handy.

Curious, I attempted to bring the phone to life by using voice commands. It would not respond. I guessed this was likely because it would be physically impossible for a cell phone from 2059 to work in 1983. I was about to stuff it into my jeans pocket when I got an idea. What if the phone wasn't responding to my voice commands because my actual voice was different? Fortunately, Denise had purchased a Holophone that possessed "classic operations mode". Simply put, *classic operations mode* allowed old, out-of-touch geezers who lacked basic tech skills, to operate the Holophone as if it were just a simple run-of-the-mill smartphone.

This time, I tapped on the phone, put in my PIN, and the phone lit up. Thankfully, due to my improved sight, I could see the screen clearly.

I had a text.

Intrigued, I brought it up. It was from an unfamiliar number and contained only one word: SUNSET.

How odd. What did it mean?

A loud voice broke my concentration.

"Billy! Get down here. It's breakfast time."

Startled, I quickly shut down the phone and stuffed it deep into my front pocket.

The voice was my mother's. It was strange to hear her familiar tone and pitch--she'd died nearly thirty years earlier.

I left my room, pounded down the stairs, and into the kitchen. Again, everything was the same as I'd remembered. The smell of freshly cooking bacon and eggs wafted into the humid air and four places were set at the wooden table in the middle of the room. My mother was standing over the stove.

I was in a perfectly recreated dream world. It felt both stunningly real and comfortable and oddly dystopian at the same time. I stood on the bottom step feeling this polar dynamic running through me.

Then, my mother turned from the stove. She was there, real, alive, in person, and just like I'd remembered.

She looked at me and wrinkled her brow.

"Billy, for God's sake, what are you staring at? Now, get along and get washed up for breakfast."

"Good morning, Mom," I said, feeling my mouth snap shut. "How are you doing today? It's so good to see you again."

She wrinkled her brow again and set her jaw like she always did.

"I declare Billy," she scolded. "What on earth has gotten into you? You're acting half-crazy. You're not sick are you?"

"Uh, no, I'm fine," I managed. "I'm just...I'll just go on and get washed up then..."

Ignoring her puzzled gaze, I quickly made my way to the bathroom.

Locking the door, I gawked into the water spotted mirror.

Thirteen-year-old Billy Kerr was staring back at me. Skinny, sandy hair, bronzed skin, and a slightly sunburned nose. I was myself inside this dream. The only thing different was that I'd retained my ninety-year-old mind--nearly 90 years of knowledge hidden inside a teenage body. The implications of this whirled around in my head. I felt like Marty McFly (1980's movie reference; Google it). Was I really young Billy Kerr again--or would I somehow run into myself somewhere in this dream? What should I do? How should I act?

I cringed as I thought about my recent interaction with my mother. It appeared as if my dream was an actual reality for her.

141

I realized that if I was going to exist in this dream world, I needed to be ordinary thirteen-year-old Billy.

I splashed some water on my face, dried off, and took a deep breath. This was going to be tenuous.

I walked into the kitchen and cautiously slid into my seat at the table.

My dad sat at one end, my mom at the other, and across from me was my sister, Nicole. They were all acting normal, but I was doing all I could to hold it together. I was actually seeing my family again! All of us together! Just like old times!

My dad, dressed in his standard button-down cotton shirt and dirty jeans, folded his rough-hewn hands, and offered a small prayer before he dug into his food.

He paid me little mind.

I gave the table a quick once over and was debating on my next move when my mom spoke.

"Did you change your clothes, Billy?"

I gawked at her and swallowed; bewildered.

"Huh?" I managed, feeling my face grow flushed.

"You were wearing that red shirt with the football on it during milking this morning--now you're in something else."

I stupidly looked down at the green John Deere T-shirt I was wearing. I didn't know what to say.

"Uh..um, I spilled something on the other one," I said weakly.

142

This seemed to placate her, and without another word, she turned her attention back to her plate. I felt my ears growing red. What the heck? I'd just gotten dressed in the clothes that'd been lying on the chair in my room. A red football shirt? Milking? Was it possible that my mother was thinking about the other Billy Kerr running around in this dream world? The one who was here before I arrived? My head was swimming. I looked over at the front door, expecting to see "other Billy" come striding in the house wearing a red shirt. Thankfully, Nicole brought back some normalcy.

"Are you going to eat anything?"

I stared across the table at her and smiled warmly. She stuck her tongue out at me.

"What are you smirking at, dork? You look like you've seen a ghost." she snarked.

I felt like getting up and giving her a hug. Dear Nicole, right there across the table, real as ever, calling me a "dork". It was simply charming!

"Cut out the bickering," my dad gruffly said, tossing a stern look at the both of us. "Finish eating so you can get to work cleaning out the chicken coop."

I turned and looked at my dad, studying his weathered face and hard eyes. I wanted to get up and give him a hug too. Tell him I loved him and that I missed him. Instead, I grabbed a couple of pieces of bacon and put them on my plate.

We all ate in silence for a moment.

Inside, I felt like a spy--secretly snooping on the previous lives of my family. It was a weird feeling, to say the least. I cautiously

143

looked at my family, a non-stop smile tugging at my lips. I couldn't contain my excitement at the moment.

"Hey, maybe we should do something special today," I blurted out. "You know--go on a picnic, hang out, and spend some quality time together as a family."

Everybody stopped eating and stared at me.

"What on earth has gotten into you, Billy Kerr?" My mother quizzed. "You've been acting strange all day."

My dad was giving me a disapproving glare, a fork full of eggs paused halfway to his mouth.

"You can hang out and spend some quality time with your sister in that dirty chicken coop," he snapped. "Now cut the nonsense and finish your breakfast."

I felt delight ripple through me. Dad was scolding me again! I hadn't experienced that in ages.

"Yeah, sure, sorry," I said, hiding the joy bouncing around inside of me.

Dad shook his head, rolled his eyes, and went back to eating.

It was the best breakfast I'd ever had. The food tasted wonderful. The atmosphere was perfect. The company around the table was exquisite.

After eating, and promising to meet Nicole in the chicken coop shortly, I retreated outside. Charley, our old blue heeler, sauntered over to greet me. I bent down and lovingly scratched him behind the ears.

"How are you doing, boy?" I asked him. "So good to see you again. You wanna take a walk with me?"

Charley just stared at me, expectant eyes, tongue out, tail wagging.

I got up and started down the driveway, feeling the orangish-brown gravel crunch under my feet. I couldn't believe the vivid texture of my dream. Everything was impeccable. I deeply breathed in the rich aroma of the farm. The smell of hay and grain mixed with the earthy smells of dirt, grit, and mud intertwined with the trace scent of diesel fuel and motor oil.

I walked past the chickens and ducks--all of them busy scratching and rooting in their pens. I stopped for a second and looked at the young calves frolicking in a pasture of aging grass. I watched as a fat pig plowed into a muddy wallow and took a contented flop in a puddle.

This amazing dream was capturing the essence of my youth and enveloping me in its grand embrace.

Then the phone in my pocket dinged.

I pulled it out. Charley looked up at me as I tapped the screen. Another text. Same phone number. One word: SUNSET.

How eerie. A second text. Sunset? What did it mean and where was it coming from? I put the phone away and looked up at the sun in the sky. Maybe I wasn't Marty McFly, maybe I was Cinderella in this fleeting dream--the charm ending once the sun dipped behind the horizon.

This thought brought a pang of distress. Everything was so perfect in this world. I didn't want to leave.

Time and its ever-present threat.

What should I do? If I only had until sunset before utopia faded, I certainly didn't want to waste my limited time cleaning a nasty old chicken coop--even if it meant spending time with my only sister.

Just then a crisp autumn breeze whistled down the driveway and the thought hit me like a hardened steel sledgehammer.

Denise!

A tingle wiggled down my spine.

Denise had to be somewhere in this dream world, right? It certainly made sense. Was it possible to see her again? The thought took my breath away. My heart began to yearn. Suddenly, that was my plan; to find Denise and see her one more time.

I looked over at the hulking chicken coop. I then looked up at the house. How could I get to Denise? I needed to go somewhere and think things over.

Thankfully, my mom was busy in the washroom. The rattling dryer dampened my entrance into the house, and I was able to quietly sneak up to my bedroom.

I sat down on my unmade bed and began to think.

The plan just seemed to appear in my mind, and in an instant, I knew what to do.

Climbing off the bed, I tiptoed across the upstairs hallway into Nicole's room. Her dark pink room was fairly neat and organized and had a flowery perfumey smell. Bruce Springsteen and Duran Duran posters were tacked on the walls, her walnut dresser was cluttered with hairpins, combs, and a curling iron. A mound of unwashed laundry was flopped on the wooden floor and teetering against the wall.

I spotted what I was looking for in the corner next to her twin bed. It was one of Nicole's most prized possessions; a bulky, boxy, black boombox (Google it). Grabbing it by the handle, I lugged it back to my room, put it on the bed, and plugged it in. Next, I opened up my closet and carelessly rooted around until I found a blue Converse shoe box. Inside, among other things, was an audio cable and a single black, 60 minute, Maxell cassette tape (Google it).

I pulled out my cell phone and prepared to wed 1980's tech with 2060's tech. Fortunately, thanks to the *classic operations mode*, my Holophone had a headphone jack (headphones generally aren't used anymore in 2059; there's something called "sensory integration" that's used--you'll just have to wait to see how it works). Anyway, I plugged one end of the audio cable into the cell phone's headphone jack, and the other ends into the LINE IN ports on Nicole's boombox. Sticking the Maxell into the cassette deck, I was now ready to make a mixtape (Google it) for Denise.

Thankfully, despite my limited interest, Denise had shown me how to download music onto my phone. I had quite an extensive library on the cell. Now, I only had to parry down a list of about 15 songs that would fit on the tape.

I finally made my selections--a mix of ballads and sentimental love songs--some of them not yet created in 1983--and slowly and painstakingly recorded them on the Maxell.

When I finished, I removed the Maxell from the boombox. There were blank labels on each side of the tape, and taking a ballpoint pen from the Converse box, I carefully wrote "From Your Secret

Admirer" on both sides. I then disconnected everything and returned Nicole's boombox.

Before leaving the upstairs, I stopped and gave my old room one last look, soaking in the memories. Something told me that this would be the last time I'd be seeing it with my own eyes; after this, it'd only exist in my memories. I stared at the Chicago Cubs logo on the calendar for just a moment and then with one last deep sigh, I turned and made my way back downstairs.

The kitchen was empty. Through the window, I could see my mother out by the clothesline with a laundry basket of whites. This was a lucky break. I quickly went to the desk in the corner of the living room and pulled out a business-sized envelope. I stuffed the Maxell inside and sealed it. On the front, I scratched *"Denise Hayes, 702 Washington Street"*. Satisfied with my work, I closed the desk and with purpose, headed for the front door.

And, that's when I ran smack dab into Nicole.

She had a red bandanna on her head, leather gloves on her hands, and dirt smeared across her face. She smelled horrible, and she was pissed. Before she noticed, I quickly stuffed the envelope into my back pocket.

"Where the HELL have you been," she snarled. "I've been out in that stinking chicken coop for two hours by myself!"

I gulped slightly and looked past her at the sun which was already on the backside of noon.

"I've been kinda busy, sis," I said.

"Don't give me that 'sis' crap you dork," she bawled, her face growing red. "You are in so much deep shit! Wait 'til dad hears about this."

My 90-year-old mind sprung into action.

"Hey, sorry," I said. "Tell you what. I'll finish up the chicken coop by myself. Why don't you just go inside and rest?"

This offer took Nicole by surprise. I could see the anger slowly fading from her face.

"You serious?"

"Yeah, absolutely," I smiled.

"No BS?"

"None," I said, holding up my hands.

"Well, OK, but you better not be trying to pull something."

"Scouts honor," I lied, looking back up at the sky. "I'll head out there right now."

Nicole seemed satisfied with the arrangement. She eagerly pulled off her gloves, threw them on the floor, and headed for the bathroom.

I watched her disappear, and when the coast was clear, I sprang out the front door.

I jogged over to the old pump house and opened the creaking door. There, inside, leaning against the wall, was my old, orange and blue bike with its duct-taped banana seat.

I backed it out of the pump house--the loose chain guard rattling like always. I climbed aboard and once again peered up into the sky.

149

Denise was fifteen miles away and I was running out of time.

I rolled out of the driveway. Old Charley stood in the yard watching me go. I pedaled up a small rise then pulled off to the side of the paved road. Looking back, I saw the farm one more time. Big white house, smaller white outbuildings, big white barn with a brown metal roof; a gravel drive snaking between the buildings.

From afar, I watched my mom, empty clothes basket under her arm, walk up and disappear into the house. Way off in the corner of the pasture I saw my dad, shovel in hand, busy digging a post hole. And, when I strained my ears, I could hear the faint melody of Duran Duran's *Hungry Like The Wolf* pumping out of Nicole's bedroom window.

I'd left the farm thousands of times in the past, but this time was the hardest. I knew that once I rolled over the top of the hill, my boyhood home would disappear from view--gone forever. For a moment I stood still, reluctant to leave.

Then I thought of Denise. It was time to go.

Denise lived in Boxer, a small Mayberryish town about fifteen miles away. I knew two ways to get there. One was on the busy two-lane highway with no shoulder, and the other was a series of less-traveled back roads. The highway was faster, but the back roads were safer. I elected to use the slower safer way.

Pedaling the bike was easier than I'd expected. My vigorous youthful legs had little trouble powering the old bike.

As I rode along through the quiet back roads, amidst the changing trees, I thought about Denise. Did she exist in this dreamscape?

Could I find her? What would she look like? Would she recognize me? What would I say to her?

It took me nearly two hours of steady pedaling to finally reach the outskirts of Boxer. My leg muscles were screaming for mercy and I had a powerful, growing thirst. I knew where the Boxer Community Park was located, so I went there first. The little park was a pleasant place full of large maples. It also had an outdoor water fountain. Parking my bike, I took a moment to get the blood flowing and then made a beeline for the water fountain. A long drink of cool water settled me and I took a deep breath. I was tempted to take a rest on one of the park benches, but my phone dinged.

Another text message. Same phone number. One word: SUNSET.

I looked up. I didn't have much time left; the sun was rapidly descending in the western sky. Time was slipping away and I had none to spare.

Getting back on my bike, I coasted down familiar Pine street and took a quick left onto the even more familiar Washington street. Down about two blocks on Washington was a square blue house. It was where Denise lived.

I felt my heart jump into my throat as I pulled up at the curb. Denise's house looked like I'd always remembered. Two stories, dark blue siding. Deck, porch, well-kept flower beds, neatly trimmed bushes, and a brown WELCOME mat placed on the concrete porch by the front door.

I'd made it.

I put the bike down next to the curb and with frayed nerves, I timidly walked up to the front door. Standing on the WELCOME mat, I paused, took a deep breath, and punched the doorbell. A

151

few moments passed before I heard shuffling from inside the house.

I was half-expecting Denise to answer the door, but when it opened there stood my mother-in-law. I recognized her but, of course, she had no idea who I was.

"Yes, can I help you?" she asked politely.

It took me a moment to gain my composure.

"Uh, hi, Mrs. Hayes...is...is Denise here?"

She squinted and a kind smile crossed her face, "Uh no, sorry, she isn't. Not right now."

My heart dropped and I felt the color drain from my face. Panic began to creep into my chest. My mother-in-law must've noticed.

"Are you one of Denise's school friends?" she asked. "You seem familiar--like we've already met. Have you been here before?"

I was flustered, "Um....no, well...yes...er...not really but sort of, I guess."

She seemed confused. "Are you OK?"

I managed to regain my composure. I gave a weak smile.

"Uh, sorry, ma'am. I'm just looking for Denise."

"Well, she's not here right now, but if you give me your name, I'll tell her you stopped by."

"Um...that's OK," I stammered stupidly, thinking about the first date I would be having with Denise about six years later. "I'll stop by sometime later."

"OK," my mother-in-law replied, puzzled. "Take care then."

I gave her a small wave and she disappeared behind the door, leaving me lost and confused on the porch.

What terrible misfortune, I thought as I dejectedly made my way back to the old bike. All the planning. All the thoughts. All the wondering. All for naught.

I looked up into the sky. The sun was barely holding above the western horizon and much like my hopes of seeing Denise, it would soon disappear into nothing.

A lump grew in my throat.

Then, I remembered the mixtape in my back pocket. This lifted my spirits a tiny bit--at least I could leave something for Denise.

I rolled across the street to the Hayes' mailbox and opened it. I dug the crumpled envelope out of my pocket and stuffed it inside. I closed the little door and was thinking about how Denise would react to the mysterious tape when I suddenly felt a profound wave of intensity ripple through my body. Suddenly, the little hairs on my forearms stood up as if they'd been electrified. Baffled by this strange aura, I looked down the street. I saw three girls walking abreast down the sidewalk. They were talking and laughing among themselves.

Still experiencing the uncanny tingling, I wheeled out further into the street for a better look.

I didn't recognize two of the girls, but the third one...the one in the middle...

And then, the very breath left my lungs. A swarm of butterflies churned up in my chest. A chilly tingle raced across my scalp and I felt like I was riding on the downslope of a giant roller coaster that was going a million miles an hour. I swallowed hard.

It was Denise; she was coming right towards me.

I stared at her, my mind going numb. She was obviously much younger, but I could see older Denise in that bouncy girl on the sidewalk. Her soft brown eyes, little dimples, and long, wavy brown hair.

As the girls got closer, I could hear Denise talking and the other two giggling at her commentary. Denise was mid-sentence when she happened to look up and see me. Instantly, our eyes locked. It was a moment of pure magic, and a pageant of emotions rocketed through me. The world seemed to pause; time stood still. Euphoria exploded like starbursts inside my chest.

Denise felt something too because her voice quietly trailed off, and her eyes widened as if she were staring into a spellbinding kaleidoscope. She focused her full attention on the young stranger sitting on a duct-taped banana bike seat.

Her two friends quickly noticed Denise's change in demeanor. Their giggling ceased and they both gave me tepid looks. One of them wrinkled her nose.

"C'mon Denise," the nose-wrinkler urged, grabbing Denise under the arm. "This is weird. Let's go."

The second girl took a cue from the first one and she grabbed Denise's other arm. Denise seemed unfazed by their rough manhandling, and as they jostled past me, she never broke her penetrating gaze.

I wanted to call out to Denise but my mouth was dry and my mind void of any rational thought. I managed nothing but a barely audible croak.

Only after the three girls disappeared into Denise's house did things seem to return to normal. The intensity that clutched me ebbed away. My jumping heart began to slow and my breath returned. I looked down at my hands. They were trembling slightly.

What now?

SUNSET.

I whirled towards the west. Just a tiny dying ray of sun remained above the horizon.

Panicked, I looked back at the house. Somebody was standing in front of the picture window.

It was Denise.

She was motionless for a moment before she gently raised her hand and waved at me. I waved back.

Then she was gone.

I woke up in my old recliner with my heart pounding wildly inside my ninety-year-old chest. I then realized that the whole thing had just been a dream.

A spate of anger rose inside of me, followed closely by profound sadness. I wanted to go back; to return to my wonderful dream. Like a fool, I closed my eyes and tried to drift back to sleep.

It was impossible. The magic dream world that held Denise was lost forever.

Defeated and desperate, I pulled myself out of the chair and limped into the kitchen to get some ibuprofen for my throbbing hip. I limped back to the chair and flipped on the TV.

Drunk in misery, I vacantly stared at the screen.

Several hours later, I woke up again. The TV was droning on and it was light outside. Once again, I struggled out of my chair and poked around in the kitchen for something to eat. I had a pathetic meal of soda crackers and sliced cheese.

Kitchen tidied up and dishes done, I went to the bedroom. I stood in the doorway for a second looking at everything I'd been avoiding.

My kids had suggested that I begin the process of organizing and downsizing. This meant the agonizing task of going through the few things still in the house that had been Denise's. I'd been adamantly opposed to doing it, but with that stupid dream fresh in my mind, I felt resigned to confronting the process.

In the end, there wasn't much to go through. A few sets of clothes, some books, knickknacks, and an assortment of jewelry. I tossed most things, minus the jewelry, into a big tote. My son could dispose of the tote; my daughter could sort the jewelry.

The very last item of Denise's was a dusty, brown file box at the back of the closet. I pulled it out, put it on the bed, and opened it up. It was full of old purses. I never understood the whole thing with purses. Why did you need more than one? Why did they have to be different sizes and colors?

Anyway, I slowly worked my way through them. Except for a few old receipts and some spare change, they were mostly empty.

The very last one was an old, beaten up, red purse that I hadn't seen in decades. I fought with the stubborn zipper for a bit before the thing finally opened. Something was inside. I pulled out the contents.

What I saw shocked and stunned me. I couldn't believe my old foggy eyes, for in my hand was a brittle, rumpled, yellowed envelope jaggedly ripped at one end. Sloppily written on the front, faded and nearly invisible was "*Denise Hayes, 702 Washington Street.*"

When I shook the envelope, an old, black Maxell cassette tape tumbled out onto the bed. The poor thing was battered, cracked, and held together with little strips of scotch tape. It had been handled so many times, the labels were nearly worn away; the words scrawled on them illegible. Only a tape that had been listened to a million times would look like this one did.

And while I was still catching my breath and contemplating the meaning of this recent discovery, my phone dinged.

 A new text.

I quickly pulled it up. Strangely, I was from Denise's old number.

One word: SUNSET.

Clutching that old Maxell in my hands, I looked out of the window into the afterglow of the rapidly approaching dusk.

Suddenly, my pain disappeared, and oddly I felt content and refreshed. A wry smile crossed my old face.

SUNSET.

Soon, I would be with her.

My Brother Dimas

There is a bitter taste in my mouth and I have a dreadful thirst as I sit here in this humid, barren place. The sky is an icky shade of yellow, the rank smell of sulfur hangs in the air, and spires of sooty black smoke regularly belch out of the fissures in the dry rocky ground. I've found no potable water.

As I sit huddled next to a thick jagged boulder, I wonder about Dimas. He should be along soon. He will stand beside me; the two of us together just like always. I'll be relieved to see him when he arrives, but eventually we'll have to have a discussion. We'll have to talk about why he chose to betray me at the end.

Dimas and I grew up together and were inseparable. When the people of the village talked about us, it was always as a pair. Dimas and Gestas did this; Dimas and Gestas did that. Dimas and Gestas got caught stealing again.

We both had bad childhoods--bad fathers to be exact--so I think that's how we ended up bonding. Like experiences always draw people together.

Barely teenagers, we left home together to seek our fortunes, and fortunes we did find, albeit the fortunes belonging to others. I guess I'll just come out and say it: Dimas and I became thieves and roadside bandits.

159

We became quite skilled at the trade. There were few better than us at waylaying some weary traveler on a desolate stretch of road. We'd generally beat the poor souls senseless and steal everything they had. It was actually a pretty good life, but Dimas just couldn't be content. He always wanted more.

Dimas had his heart set on making a big score--rob some ultra-rich person--and set us up for life.

I was reluctant to go along with this idea at the beginning. I knew the authorities did little to remedy the problems of some unfortunate pilgrim who was accosted by a couple of small-time highwaymen. But robbing a rich important member of society? That'd bring out the authorities faster than stink on a camel. Dimas didn't listen to my reason. He said we were accomplished thieves and we'd have little trouble pulling off a sizable robbery. He kept broaching the subject, and over time the idea grew on me.

We selected some pompous rich guy's house to do the deed. What a treasure trove was inside! I'd never seen such opulence; so many things; so much gold.

Things were going handsomely until that kid walked in.

I imagine he was about twelve-years-old. He just kind of idly wandered into the bedroom Dimas and I were ransacking. Truthfully, I didn't hear him coming and he startled me. I paused for a moment and just stared at him. Thick black hair, wide brown eyes, olive skin; dressed in a colorful linen garment and expensive sandals. He seemed startled too and I saw him trying to comprehend what was happening. Then Dimas hit him.

Dimas hit him hard--violently hard on the head--and with a sad grunt, the kid toppled to the floor. I'd never seen so much blood in my life. It positively gushed out of his cracked head.

Dimas and I split immediately, taking our ill-gotten gains with us.

We hid in a cave in the foothills that night. Dimas seemed obsessed with all the gold, jewels, and utensils we'd stolen. I didn't share his excitement; I couldn't get the image of that rumpled bleeding kid out of my mind.

I tried to talk to Dimas about it, but he didn't seem concerned. He said something like that was bound to happen, it was unfortunate, but it was the price of doing business. I put the incident out of my mind after that.

Then, the bottom fell out of our lives. We were coming out of the foothills one day when we found ourselves suddenly surrounded by a company of soldiers. Turns out the house we robbed was that of a prominent senator. Turns out the kid was his only son. Turns out the kid died.

When the soldiers searched us, they found a couple of rings that belonged to the senator. We were caught red-handed.

They roughly shackled us and tossed us into prison. Sitting in that rank, damp hellhole, I had a lot of time to reflect on my life. A fit of deep resentful anger began to burn inside me. The world had been unfair to Dimas and me. We were forced to live hard-luck lives. Ruined childhoods. Lack of social structure. Nobody to depend on. Nobody that loved us. We only ever had each other and did the best we could with the life we'd been handed.

As if others could've done better given the same set of circumstances.

I was astounded at the uproar that the death of the senator's son caused. People would come down to the prison to get a look at the two degenerates who killed an innocent kid.

I remember one well-heeled dignitary stared at us with disgust and proclaimed that our barbarism was on par with that of Barabbas.

Barabbas? Were we really on the same level with that fiend?

Apparently we were and after a quick sham of a trial, Dimas and I were sentenced to death by crucifixion. We waited in the prison for our sentence to be carried out. Neither of us said much. We were both resigned to our fate, and as always, like brothers, we would face things together.

On our execution day, they led us to a grim nasty place outside of the city appropriately called *the place of the skull.*

I was surprised that there were three crosses waiting on that hill of death. Apparently, another condemned man was to die with us.

I soon learned that the other guy was a weak-minded chap named Jesus who'd been going around the countryside the last few years making bold claims of his identity, contending he was the Messiah of all things! Unlike us, he hadn't killed anybody, precipitated an uprising, or committed any violent offense, but he'd ran afoul a bunch of powerful people and was about to pay for it with his life.

Some people felt sorry for this guy, but I wasn't one of them. It irked me that a contingent of his misguided followers, wailing and crying, had accompanied him to his death while Dimas and I faced our fate alone. Even more infuriating was that the guy could've saved himself if he would've just retracted his inflammatory rhetoric-- but he refused. It seemed like this charlatan was intent on dying at all costs. It was pathetic. Just recant some of the wild claims, eat a little crow, and go free! Why be so stubborn?

If he wanted to die so bad, I wished he would take my place--die in my stead--so I could go free.

They put me and Dimas up first. I don't remember it, I passed out from the pain. When I came around, through my groggy eyes, I saw that Dimas and I had been separated; Jesus, king of the Jews, had been placed in between us on his cross.

This was the final straw for me. If I had to die, I wanted to die next to my only friend, my only brother, the only one in the world that I could trust. But, no, this usurper, this grifter, was placed in between us.

The distinguished leaders, on the ground below us, appeared to harbor similar feelings. They called out to this Jesus asking him to save himself if he was indeed the Chosen One.

Although it was painful, I turned and smirked at him. The people below had a point. If he was such a wunderkind why didn't he save himself? Truth was that he couldn't save anybody.

Feeling a swell of hate grow inside of me, I looked at him.

"Aren't you the Messiah? Save yourself and us."

He did not reply. Typical.

I was contemplating what else to say when something strange happened.

It was Dimas, my dear brother, who spoke for the first time.

"Don't you fear God since you are undergoing the same punishment," he asked me. "We are punished justly because we're getting back what we deserve for the things we did, but this man has done nothing wrong."

Dimas' word stung. Where did that train of thought come from? It made no sense. I couldn't believe he was chiding me; contradicting me. He'd never done that before.

Dimas did not address me again. Instead in a patently pleading voice, he spoke directly to the fake Messiah hanging between us.

"Jesus, remember me when you come into your kingdom."

I have to give this Jesus guy credit because he kept his ruse up even on the cross. He turned to my friend.

"Truly I tell you, today you will be with me in paradise."

I scoffed at this. Perhaps Dimas had lost his mind due to the pain. Perhaps, this Jesus was trying to somehow offer my friend some misplaced comfort. But, I was not going to be fooled by this man.

I drifted away.

Now here I was in this place, and like a loyal brother, I would wait until Dimas arrived. We would navigate this strange new world together and nobody would tear us apart.

About The Author

The author of three previous novels, John Lory currently lives in Central Wisconsin with his wife and two children. Waiting At The Dock is his first collection of short stories.

Made in the USA
Columbia, SC
11 February 2021